No Man's Land

OTHER HENRY HOLT NOVELS
BY MARTIN WALSER

TRANSLATED BY LEILA VENNEWITZ

Runaway Horse
The Swan Villa
The Inner Man
Letter to Lord Liszt
Breakers

No Man's Land

A NOVEL BY
MARTIN WALSER

TRANSLATED FROM THE GERMAN BY
LEILA VENNEWITZ

HENRY HOLT AND COMPANY
NEW YORK

Originally published in the Federal Republic of Germany
under the title *Dorle und Wolf.*

The translation of passages from Friedrich Schiller's *Die
Jungfrau von Orleans* is by an anonymous translator.

Library of Congress Cataloging-in-Publication Data
Walser, Martin, 1927–
No man's land.
Translation of: Dorle und Wolf.
I. Title.
PT2685.A48D6713   1989   833'.914   89-9151
ISBN 0-8050-0667-2

Henry Holt books are available at special discounts for bulk
purchases for sales promotions, premiums, fund-raising, or
educational use. Special editions or book excerpts can also be
created to specification.

For details, contact:

Special Sales Director
Henry Holt and Company, Inc.
115 West 18th Street
New York, New York 10011

First American Edition

Designed by Susan Hood
Printed in the United States of America
1   3   5   7   9   10   8   6   4   2

TRANSLATOR'S ACKNOWLEDGMENT

I am happy to express my deep gratitude to my husband, William, for his unstinting and invaluable assistance throughout the work of this translation.

Leila Vennewitz

TRANSLATOR'S NOTE

At the end of World War II, the victorious Allies divided the defeated German nation into four zones of occupation. The Eastern, Soviet-occupied zone eventually became the German Democratic Republic (GDR) and a member of the Soviet bloc, while the three zones occupied by the Western Allies became the Federal Republic of Germany (FRG) and a member of NATO.

In 1963 a wall was erected by East Germany along its western border, effectively preventing travel and other interchange between the two states.

Many Germans living in the two Germanys have not been able to reconcile themselves to the partition. In this story Martin Walser tells us about one of them.

No Man's Land

1

IF YOU HAVE something to hide you must do more than you yourself would consider necessary. Although Wolf knew no one was watching him, he behaved as if he had to convince someone who was constantly watching him that he was harmless. He would, for instance, often whistle to himself. After getting off the bus he would take the trouble to cross Trierer-Strasse, a street not all that easy to cross, pause on the other side in front of the florist's window, and gaze with obvious fondness at the potted plants displayed along the sidewalk. He hoped to be taken for a flower lover. If he was being watched. But then he wasn't being watched at all. Perhaps, as Dorle's husband, he had at some time or other been the object of a so-called security check. For a while he had suspected Mr. Ujfalussy, who lived on the same floor, of being an informer; but in fact he really was only a mathematician. And a bachelor. That he was.

Today Wolf even bought something at the florist's. Not because that was what a flower lover was expected to do, but because it was Dorle's birthday. He bought a phalaenopsis and walked back across Trierer-Strasse, carrying the white blossom, which was much too large for its long stem, as if through a storm. Today he almost did wish he was being watched. On the side street that goes off from Trierer-Strasse just before Number 47, he saw Dorle's car.

Dorle was busy in the kitchen. Reaching around her, he set the phalaenopsis down in front of her. Dorle made a sound as if in some blissful pain. "Happy thirty-fifth birthday," he said, "and if you have no objection I'll love you as much as ever or even more." She had no objection, said Dorle. "As much as ever or even more?" Wolf asked. Dorle: "Even more, if you don't mind."

He led her out of the kitchen into the bedroom, made her stand in front of the big mirror, himself behind her, and placed his gift of jewelry around her neck. Two golden bands that curved apart on either side of a green stone to join again below the stone. American, the salesman had said, about 1905. In any case, beautiful. When the necklace was in place, Dorle uttered an even more fervent little cry of pain. For weeks Wolf had broken his journey home from Schlegel-Strasse at the railway station and walked all over town until he had found this piece. He would rather have confessed to finding nothing than have bought something that hadn't unreservedly pleased him. Dorle stood there for a little while with his arm around her. Together they looked into the mirror, gazing at the necklace and at one another. "How can anything be so beautiful?" said Wolf. "Off to the kitchen," said Dorle. "Dr. Meissner and his wife are coming at eight thirty."

2

Wolf showered, changed, and offered to make the salad. But at seven he had to leave the kitchen again, switch on the radio to short wave, and take the decoding block out of the mattress. By the time the last of the Brahms *Four Serious Songs* came on, he was seated in front of the set. Then came his number, 17–11–21, followed by the figures that he jotted down and decoded. Finally he came into the kitchen with three slips of paper. He was quite excited: the general had sent Dorle his best wishes for her birthday! Dorle was not pleased; she was scared. That was how the Guillaumes had been blown, she said. Birthday wishes for the recipient's wife! They know the code! So the computer is asked who among all the civil servants in Bonn has a wife with a birthday today! Wolf said his code was impossible to crack because the same one was never used twice. He was proud of his invention, the sliding code. Only he and a single coder on Normannen-Strasse in East Berlin knew the system Wolf had worked out.

But Dorle would not be reassured. "I know," said Wolf, as he gave her a big hug. He was much too weak. He couldn't protect Dorle. He needed luck; without luck he was done for. Anyone who needs luck is done for. Not he. He wasn't done for. It was just that there are moments when one begins to tremble, when one is overcome by the feeling that the world might come crashing down any second and is about to do just that. If Dorle only knew how weak he was! That was something she must never find out. Never.

"Did you have a nice birthday party at the office?" he asked. Dorle said that once again Sylvia Wellershoff had behaved atrociously. She had demanded her third piece of cake from the still-uncut strawberry cake. Dr. Meissner, who was in charge of the cutting, hadn't wanted to cut into the strawberry cake just for a single piece, since it was almost five o'clock and everyone had already had two pieces. "But I want some of that one!" Sylvia had insisted. Dr. Meissner had looked beseechingly at Dorle. Dorle had said: "Some people have to have something of everything," whereupon Sylvia had retorted: "She begrudges me everything, does our little South German!" Whereupon Dorle: "*Southwest* German, if you don't mind!" It had been terrible.

What Dorle had to tell was anything but terrible. But for Dorle everything Sylvia did was terrible. Sylvia looked for opportunities to be terrible in Dorle's eyes. He ought to smack Sylvia. How else was he to make her leave Dorle alone? Each time he was with Sylvia she promised to avoid Dorle, to spare her, never again to do anything that might hurt her. But again and again she had to assert herself, had to let Dorle feel she had power over Wolf. She probably suspected that he told Dorle he only went to Sylvia because she supplied him with copies of protocols. And actually that was his only reason. Sylvia, however, believed that there was more between them. And she had to let Dorle feel this. No one has ever been known to refrain from exerting power.

"I'm sorry," said Dorle.

That was the worst: she apologized to him! If anyone had to apologize . . . But he couldn't say that. He showed her the second slip of paper. He has been promoted. He's now a major in the National People's Army. "Oh," she said. "Oh, Wolf!" she said. She congratulated him. "That's my reward for MRS 903," said Wolf. But there's more: he must go down at once to the phone booth and call that odious Dr. Bruno. Make him toe the line. He was working himself to death, said Dorle, for a promotion from which he had nothing to gain. Now he tried to look sad. He wanted her to notice that. His reaction implied that, even when his work here was done, she wouldn't accompany him across the border. She said again: "I'm sorry." She was a bit on edge today, she said. Just before five Dr. Meissner had been summoned to the minister's office. Before going up he had asked her to wait until he came back. Then she had had to follow him right into his office. Leave the birthday party. He had asked her whether she would care to go to Brussels with him, in two weeks' time. "To the NATO conference," said Wolf. Before going to see the minister, Dorle went on, Dr. Meissner had hinted at how much he would like her to accompany him to Brussels; after seeing the minister he had made no further mention of it. He had come back quite changed. Dazed, somehow, or bewildered, or . . .

"Hold it!" said Wolf. "We're not permitted to let our imaginations run wild in this direction, you know that! Suppose I were to tell you: the new minister, a month in office, summons Dr. Meissner and confronts him with all his shortcomings—new brooms, and so on. Please, Dorle, no fear fantasies. We're beyond that now, after nine years of unblemished activity. But this Brussels meeting was point number three of today's message. They need the protocol. Right on the heels of the Copenhagen conference, yet another one. In East Berlin they suspect it's about the camouflage technology of 'Stealth.' Just imagine—NATO has an invisible aircraft, not detectable by any radar! What can't they do to us with that! All the electronic stuff we've sent across so far is wasted if NATO can blow everything to bits with an invisible fighter-bomber. I'm sorry, Dorle, you'd rather not know anything about it. Look, the very first day they've caught up over there I'm calling it quits, you know that. But as long as they haven't emerged from the electronic Stone Age . . ." He waited for her to agree. A nod would have been enough. Dorle did not nod.

"Until today Dr. Meissner wanted me to go with him," she said. "His wife is again in her eighth month." Dorle couldn't get over the fact that, after seeing the minister, Dr. Meissner had said nothing more about Brussels. She wouldn't have gone anyway. She would have suggested Sylvia again. Wolf said: "Or you could go after all." Dorle: "Or Hildegard." In this way Dorle forced him to admit that he knew quite a bit about Sylvia, even had some sort of hold over her, because, if she refused to play anymore, he could inform Dominick, her husband, who, it seemed, was a rather shady character. Besides, Sylvia believed—and this meant there were no problems in his relationship with her—that Wolf was, well, how should she put it, sexually in her thrall.

That was why Sylvia was always so cheeky to her, said Dorle.

Sylvia was the least of their worries, said Wolf. "If you take on the job instead of Sylvia, you'll be one of us. For the first time."

"The fact that Dr. Meissner might take advantage of an opportunity like Brussels doesn't bother you," said
Dorle.

"That's your business," he said.

"My God, what a strict Prussian you are!" exclaimed Dorle.

Wolf, as casually as possible: "You can rely on a Prussian. Doesn't that count for something?"

"It counts for a lot, Wolf," she replied. "It counts for more than anything."

He felt as if he had blackmailed her.

All the time they had been talking he had been fixing the salad. "All I need now are the artichoke hearts," he said. Dorle said there hadn't been any fresh ones. "And my genius for spontaneity hates cans," said Wolf as he drew her to him. Very softly and without emphasis and rather quickly she said she was thirty-five, after all, it was already a bit late for child-bearing, she was just mentioning it, but once a year she must be allowed to mention it, that again he wouldn't . . . right?

Wolf nodded and left.

2

To WHAT EXTENT may one's thoughts contradict one's actions? How much irreconcilability can one bear within oneself? Whenever Wolf went down to the phone booth at the edge of Poppelsdorf he had to ask himself why he didn't make these phone calls from his home although he was sure his line wasn't tapped.

By the time he arrived at the phone booth he had reduced his state of mind to a formula: Behave like someone under strict surveillance but be aware that there is not the slightest reason to do so. The booth was occupied. By a Turk, a guest worker. By the very prototype of a Turk. The man was laughing, dazzling teeth under a glossy mustache. Although he was facing Wolf, looking out, looking at Wolf, it was a safe bet he didn't see him. A perfect demonstration of the fact that one sees only what one wants to see. If he would at least turn away, show some embarrassment! It was almost insulting to be overlooked in this way. The man was laughing, prancing about. What words were being spoken into that ear? Wolf could feel his rage mounting in him. Was it envy or impatience? Or were his nerves simply not strong enough? The best thing would be for him to envy this colorful fellow his colors and his vitality. He was alive. And right now. At this very moment. No one could be in sharper contrast to himself.

When the man finished his talking and laughing and bodily contortions and finally emerged, he walked past Wolf without noticing him. So Wolf had no chance to throw him a thoroughly dirty look.

Well then, Dr. Bruno, now it's your turn. But Dr. Bruno answered in a voice that sounded as if he were being made to lift a hundred-kilo weight. Wolf refused to be impressed. "York speaking," he snapped. "Let's make it short, Dr. Bruno: On July first the 750-thousand-franc credit with the Union Bank of Switzerland will expire. Which means Nortel wishes to have the rest of MRS 903 in the Nortel display at the electronics fair at Budapest by June twenty-sixth. . . ." "Just a moment, Mr. York!" cried the panting Dr. Bruno. "I'm still waiting for the money for Options 1 and 4!" But now Wolf was shouting. "How stupid do you think my customers are?" he yelled. "Until Options 2 and 3 of the 903 equipment arrive at Nortel, everything delivered to date is junk!"

Dr. Bruno said no more. But his breathing was so loud and labored that Wolf saw himself obliged to change his tone. By the time Wolf left the phone booth he was sweating. Dr. Bruno had promised to deliver Options 2 and 3. As far as Basel. No farther. From California to the Netherlands and from there to Basel. That would be difficult enough. The firm in Holland, or rather the man in that firm whom he had persuaded with a lot of money to sign as end user, was not prepared to ship to the Eastern bloc. Basel, and that was it. Again and again Dr. Bruno had simply resorted to his labored, loud breathing. According to his doctor, he should be dealing only in feathers, Dr. Bruno had said. Wolf had shouted loud, empty threats into the phone. Dr. Bruno had breathed heavily. Wolf had had to tone down. Probably he was simply barking up the wrong tree. Somehow he had to get around this Dr. Bruno and onto the Dutch supplier who was obtaining the goods from California.

As Wolf passed the bus stop on his way home, he noticed a man who had been standing there when Wolf had walked by earlier. But meanwhile at least two buses had stopped here on their way into town. Wolf decided to sit down on the bench and stay there until this man got on a bus. Two women were sitting on the bench. As Wolf sat down, one woman was telling the other that she had been arrested the night before, in the Eastern zone. That's right! And only then did she say she had dreamed it. Wolf pretended to have changed his mind. It was a mistake anyway to wait until that man boarded a bus. That would only prove to him that Wolf knew he was being watched. Then they would follow him even more carefully. In any case, move on now. Home. Probably the man had a date, was waiting for a nurse from one of the clinics on the Venusberg. She was supposed to turn up on one of the buses. And didn't. That was all. But if Wolf was the object of a security check as the husband of a secretary employed at the Ministry of Defense, then he had just drawn suspicion upon himself. He sure had. They know the Ziegers have a phone in their home. So why does Mr. Zieger go to a phone booth? His number hasn't been disconnected because of unpaid bills. So . . .

Normally he always made these calls from town. But today, the birthday, Dr. Meissner and wife . . . Still, it was a mistake. And *one* mistake is enough. A single one. Just as in chess. As everywhere. He also had to fight off the notion that that woman had told her Eastern-zone arrest dream solely for his benefit.

3

Dr. Meissner and his wife had already arrived by the time Wolf came home. When Wolf saw the pregnant Mrs. Meissner he knew that Dorle couldn't look forward to a pleasant evening. And in fact Mrs. Meissner did and said almost nothing that wasn't somehow connected with her pregnancy. On accepting a second helping she said: "The little fellow's insatiable again today!" On refusing wine she said she was glad to go without alcohol for the little fellow's sake. Because she referred to the little fellow as if he were already there, Dorle couldn't refrain from asking whether the sex of the child had already been established. No, not exactly, but since they already have three boys and tend to be conservative, too, the fourth child is bound to be another boy.

Wolf was tempted to say that he had recently read something about the super-fetation of rabbits. If he remembered rightly, they ovulated again thirty-six days after bearing a litter, but they gave birth after forty-two days, which meant that the next gestation had already started and, if there were no new sperm, with old stored-up or left-over sperm. He couldn't get it quite straight in his mind. But maybe Dorle wouldn't have approved of this attempt to react to the Meissners' procreative zeal.

Dr. Meissner sipped and swallowed and praised the Roussillon. Wolf drank beer. Dr. Meissner expressed his pleasure that Dorle and he were the only wine drinkers. Where had they found this lovely red wine? Dorle explained that her brother had a house in the southwest of France—to be more specific, an old tower in the Têt valley—that was where this wine came from. Dr. Meissner wanted to know the price. The exact price. He was constantly on the lookout for good red wines. Since he was the son of an alcoholic mother, he said, that was not surprising. "Now Jürgen, don't be so boastful!" said his wife. "Eat up that nice mousse, Nina," he said. "Your little fellow's still hungry." If there was anything in this lethal world that allowed him still to believe in good, it was the marvel of motherhood, he went on. "Dorle, it's about time for you, too!" he said. And when Dorle didn't react immediately, he continued: "You would really be an excellent mother, I can sense that." Dorle replied that she and Wolf hadn't quite reached that point yet. Wolf, in a tone of finality: "But soon, Dr. Meissner."

Now that Nina had really cleaned up her plate, Wolf took out a cigarette and offered one to Dorle. "May we?" he asked. "Oh," said Mrs. Meissner, "you want to smoke . . . not that I mind, but the little fellow doesn't like it, I can feel that." Whenever she mentioned her little fellow she tapped her bulging stomach. Dr. Meissner said: "Dorle is now the last remaining smoker in Section 211, Mr. Zieger!"

Wolf remarked that his influence on Dorle was the

worst imaginable. Then he asked Dorle whether she'd like a quick smoke outside. Dorle replied that the longer one postpones something the more attractive it becomes. "How true!" said Dr. Meissner, eyeing Dorle rapturously. Wolf said that unfortunately he couldn't wait. "You'll excuse me," he said. But where did he intend to go, cried Mrs. Meissner? Did they have a balcony? No, they didn't. He could smoke in the kitchen. And he was gone. Furious. He heard Dr. Meissner call out after him: "Take your time! I love being alone with my two favorite women!" Since the doors were open, he could hear Dr. Meissner proceed to comment on the apartment. It was really time the Ziegers got out of here. Was it Dorle's Swabian thrift or the Spartan nature of her East German husband that made them stay on here? Both, said Dorle. Her boss commended them for saving up for a place of their own. Did they already have something in mind? In St. Augustin, said Dorle. "Wonderful!" he cried. "We'll be getting closer, Dorle!" "Over my dead body," said his wife. "Might be interesting," he said.

The phone rang: it was Dieter, Dorle's brother. He was calling from his car, on his way back from Holland, just nearing the border. He'd drop in for a moment. The Meissners said it was time for them to leave anyway. But Wolf was already back and pouring more red wine. Dr. Meissner drank the way a hungry man eats. He could afford to do this since he had an absolutely dry chauffeur. "Dorle, here's to your birthday! The best of luck to you!" Dorle drank, too. How long had Wolf been over here now, he asked? Nearly fifteen years. "Fifteen years beside the Rhine and still drinking beer!" cried Dr. Meissner and drank. He had been here for twenty-two years.

But when he and Nina were driving away from Jena for the very last time, on their way out of East Germany, what had he said at the time, Nina? That he would never get away from Jena, that's what he'd said, Nina replied. "How true," he said. "Your native soil, you know—even the reality of socialism can't destroy something like one's native soil." Did Wolf still have anyone over there? His father, said Wolf. Well then, Wolf knew what it meant. Wolf said that unfortunately he couldn't go there anymore. "You should be glad," said Dr. Meissner and went on talking about himself. Six weeks ago he had buried his mother, over there in Jena, she was an alcoholic—no question, Nina, that was the only reason she stayed over there. She knew for sure that her son would have placed her in a withdrawal center until she dried out.

Now Nina cut in: It was simply that his mother had been much better cared for over there. The neighbors couldn't do enough for her because they each hoped to get her house. "And now some Party bigwig has it after all," said Dr. Meissner. For days the Meissners tried to find out who had really been the nicest of all to his mother. One does want to be fair, doesn't one? So: Mr. Heinz Klein, an engineer in the Agromachinery Combine not only ingratiated himself with his mother but also did all her repairs, and he has four kids too and lives in three tiny rooms—so he's the one who should have it, so he gets it, but hardly does he have it than a professor of Marxism-Leninism appears on the scene demanding that Mr. Klein sell the house to him immediately—if not he would see to it that Mr. Klein wouldn't be allowed to move in. And he gets it. One often sees this with animals. When a weak one gets hold of something but hasn't swallowed it yet, a stronger one comes and snatches the prey from the weaker one's mouth.

"The jokes, Jürgen!" cried Nina. Jürgen must tell the Ziegers the jokes told them by Mr. Klein the engineer. Dr. Meissner, who the more he drank the more he slipped into a Rhenish accent, now switched to a straight Thuringian-Saxon dialect. "What's the difference between *Pravda* and *Neues Deutschland? Pravda* costs ten pfennigs, *Neues Deutschland* fifteen. The five pfennigs are for the translation!" Both Meissners erupted into gales of laughter. Wolf and Dorle couldn't equal that. Then Dr. Meissner struggled out of his paroxysm so he could tell the next joke.

At last year's COMECON conference the Russian delegate had proposed: "Let us share everything we have produced in brotherly fashion." And a Pole immediately yells: "No way—fifty-fifty!" Nina, through her own laughter: "Oh, and the one about the sun, Jürgen!" "Yes," he cries, "yes, that's the best of the lot! So here goes: In the morning the sun shines into Honecker's study and says: 'Good morning, Mr. Chairman, I hope you slept well.' At noon the sun says: 'Hullo, Mr. Honecker, I hope you've had a good morning.' In the evening it says: 'Asshole!' Why? Because by this time it's crossed the border into the West!" Even Dorle had to laugh now. Wolf actually laughed the loudest, but his laugh wasn't quite as easy as Meissner's and Dorle's.

When the laughter had finally subsided, Dr. Meissner asked: "When was the last time you were over there?" But before Wolf could answer, Mrs. Meissner said: "Jürgen! You've already asked that. Mr. Zieger can't go across at all anymore, poor man." Wolf said: "I once got into some trouble over there, actually I'd quite like to tell you about it because I didn't say anything about it when I first came over here. And sometimes that can weigh on a person. I wouldn't have thought that a suppressed episode in one's life history could make itself felt for so long." He could hardly wait to hear it, said Dr. Meissner.

Oh well, it was no big deal, Wolf continued: he had slapped his professor. In Leipzig. He'd been studying piano with him, for a year, then when he had to perform for him the professor had made fun of his playing—he didn't criticize, just made fun of it. A week later there's a concert in the little Gohlis Schloss, a Polish pianist; after the concert Wolf lies in wait for his professor and slaps his face. The professor falls awkwardly. Massive concussion, so Wolf clears out, over the border. But he says nothing about this affair at the refugee reception center. He's afraid they'll extradite him. He makes out that he's been studying law for a year. He'd wanted to do that anyway. He hadn't the makings of a pianist. The professor had been right. But at the time Wolf hadn't been able to swallow that.

Dr. Meissner advised him to supply this additional information—to the head of his department. God only knew what could result from such harmless suppressions. The trouble was, said Wolf, that his professor had been a dissident, whereas Wolf had been looked upon more or less with favor. Wolf's father had been in Buchenwald with Thälmann. But had survived. Naturally he had also suppressed this fact at the refugee reception center in Giessen, otherwise they would have been even more suspicious of him. He had simply wanted to offer

17

a life history containing a minimum of inconsistencies. In other words, present himself as the prototype of a refugee from the German Democratic Republic.

All the more important, maintained Dr. Meissner, to admit the inconsistencies frankly now. In his case it had been the reverse. Too much bourgeoisie. His father a big shot at the Zeiss works. . . . "In short, the prototype of a refugee from the German Democratic Republic," said Meissner's wife. "I'm sorry to interrupt, Jürgen, it's the little fellow—none of the others ever bullied me like this! That sausage over there in the little basket, it looks so absolutely delicious, like a glossy ad. . . ." "That means she's hungry again," said Dr. Meissner. Dorle was already bringing the sausage to the table. From her brother, she said, who had a sausage factory. He had always made such good sausages that eventually he'd had to turn his butcher shop into a factory. Wolf insisted that the Meissners take one of these sausages home; he and Dorle couldn't possibly get through them all. "Because there are no kids!" cried Dr. Meissner. "Our three rascals would polish off a sausage like that in no time!" Nina, eating: "And the fourth isn't shy about helping himself either!"

Dr. Meissner began to philosophize. Of course, people without kids don't know what they're missing. . . . Wolf, holding the bottle over Meissner's glass, said: "May I?" "You must!" cried Dr. Meissner. "If I came from around here I'd say: You ought to be ashamed of yourself! Because you're still drinking beer!" And he raised his glass to Dorle. That explained why Zieger was so skinny, too—he didn't drink enough. "You look as though you weren't properly climatized yet!" cried Dr. Meissner. "Acclimatized," said Mrs. Meissner. "Same thing," he said. Or was Mr. Zieger working too hard? What did he do, anyway? He was with the Baden-Württemberg delegation in Bonn, said Wolf, Commerce and Publicity. Oh yes, Meissner had heard that somewhere. "But what do you really do?" Wolf could feel a knot forming in his stomach. Oh, he said as offhandedly as possible, it was his job to see that the political work of such a delegation didn't degenerate into a legalistic bulwark for an unproductive bureaucracy.

"Instead?" asked Dr. Meissner.

As one American had put it, said Wolf: Rendering white-collar workers productive was the great challenge of the century.

"But how?" cried Dr. Meissner. "How?"

"Do you really want to know?" asked Wolf in an almost threatening voice. Dr. Meissner did. Wolf recited his text, very fast, his voice even but not droning. Simply without pity. Based on American management theories, he said, he was trying to develop a "critical path" for his office. In other words: the implementing of well-known optimalization procedures to achieve an ever-transparent administration of productivity. The administration must be rendered receptive to its task: the realization of policy. He supported neither the Harzburg nor the St. Gallen model. Management by objectives, that was his bag. He was a follower of Klaus Zeemann's—Dr. Meissner would know about him—who claimed that, while it may be possible to have Management By Objectives without Program Budget Techniques, there can be no PBT without MBO. Zeemann was fond of quoting Colonel-General Ludwig Beck, chief of the General Staff, who was executed on July 20, 1944: "Anyone wishing to gain the confidence of others and, particularly in times of crisis, keep it, must also have a great soul." They were living in times of crisis with no end in sight. As a result of the partition of Germany. A political administration that is no longer aware of this was nothing but a meaningless bureaucracy. Each individual civil servant must be aware of the duty of his office. Self-actualization plus job-satisfaction is tantamount to effectualization in terms of the value system described by our constitution. Since the others said nothing, he added: "That's all it is."

Dr. Meissner had already drunk too much to be able to follow him. "I see," he said, "sounds just fine, actually. He's ambitious, isn't he, Dorle!" "Tremendously, Dr. Meissner," Dorle replied.

Dr. Meissner: "That's why he's so skinny!"

Dr. Meissner laughed and raised his glass to Dorle. Did they know what had upset him most during his visit to East Germany? The towels. In the hotels. They were incapable of absorbing water or moisture. Which means that the ability to produce terry cloth has been lost over there. "So I ask you, granted our East German brothers need to have their hotel towers built by Japanese and Swedes, but terry cloth, I ask you! If terry cloth can be lost, where will it all end?" He fell silent, profoundly upset. The tragic silence was broken by Nina's voice: "But Jürgen, we didn't stay in a hotel, and in private homes . . ."

"Oh, Nina!" he cried. "Believe me, I do keep my eyes and ears open before making such a sweeping statement. On German soil, no more terry cloth."

The doorbell rang. Dorle's brother. Wolf ushered him

in. Mrs. Meissner said: "Come along, let's go, husband."
Dorle introduced her brother. Dieter Beuerle. "Beuerle,"
said Dr. Meissner, "how very nice! With ä-u or e-u?"
"With e-u," replied Dieter. "With e-u, Nina," said Dr.
Meissner, "we must remember that." As he was leaving,
another joke occurred to him. "D'you know the one, Mr.
Zieger, about the workers asking one another: 'What's
your idea of happiness?' The American worker says:
'Happiness is a snazzy convertible, a good-looking wife,
and a home of my own with a patio!' The Frenchman:
'A good wife, a snappy girlfriend, and a good dinner waiting for me every day.' The East German: 'When I'm
home alone Saturday afternoon, it's raining outside, it's
snug and warm inside, there's a ring at the door, I open
up, there's a guy standing there in a trench coat and a
hat and he gives me a look and says: Are you Mr. Müller?
And then I can say: No, that's the fellow upstairs, one
floor up.' " Once again Meissner laughed the loudest at
his own joke. "We've left all that behind, haven't we,
Mr. Zieger?" he said. "Yes," said Wolf, "thank God."

On his way to the stairs Dr. Meissner bent down
quickly to the nameplate of the other apartment on the
same floor. "Look at that!" he said, and spelled out the
name loudly and laboriously and, Wolf felt, trium-
phantly, as if he had made a discovery: Tamás Ujfalussy.
"I wonder where he's from?" he asked. "Hungary," said
Wolf. "At the very least," said Dr. Meissner. Wolf coun-
tered with: "A mathematician." "Aha!" cried Dr. Meissner. And Wolf gleefully: "At the University of Bonn."
"Even so, Zieger, believe me, you must get out of here,"
said Dr. Meissner. Dorle and he were entitled to very   21
favorable loans. He'd figure it out for them sometime.

And his wife: "You can take him up on that. Financing—that's his passion."

When Wolf came back, Dorle was smoking, too. Dieter told them he had only dropped by to make it crystal clear that Dorle and Wolf must quit their jobs immediately. They must move at latest this fall. With him they would earn ten times as much. "He says that," says Dorle, "without asking first how much we're earning here." "Ten times as much with me," persisted Dieter. He's working his head off, never a week under ninety hours, for certain things he simply doesn't want to take on any outsiders. He refuses to be put off any longer. He's bought a house for them. In Strümpfelbach. Dorle exclaimed: "In Strümpfelbach, Wolf!" "Built 1930," Dieter went on, "the lot is almost half an acre, with mature trees, there's even a little cast-iron fountain. You must give notice tomorrow." He'll make at least as good a boss as that Dr. Meissner. And with him they'd have a share in the business. After three years, if they don't annoy him too much, 5 percent participation, after six years 10 percent and so on. After eighteen years they'll own 30 percent. No argument. He's already drawn up the papers. Here they are. They can study them. He'll phone tomorrow evening. "Don't be so stubborn, Wolf. I'd sure like to know what your objections are!" But now he must be off. At night the autobahn is still worthwhile. In three hours he'll be home. Half an hour before Rosi expects him. "It's this half hour that I come home too early that makes her like me." So, tomorrow he expects an answer. It'd better be positive! Goodnight, brother-in-law! Sweet dreams, little sister!

When they were alone, Wolf sat down at the piano and softly played first the left hand, then the right, of

Schumann's *Novellettes*. He always played with only one hand. That was part of his excessive caution. One must do more than one considers necessary. While he was tracing the Schumann rhythms, first one hand then the other, he said: "That stupid asshole with his sickening jokes. Farting about his native soil. No, no, no. If I were ever to lose faith, a Dr. Meissner would be enough to bring me back in line again. Do you think he was trying to egg me on? He's had me checked out, after all. Husband of a woman who has access to confidential level 'Cosmic.' I'm really pleased now, Dorle. It was an important evening. If—and I can hardly imagine this—they have found out about my slapping Geschwendner and my lie about studying law for a year—we're free. I've told everything. So he can pass it on tomorrow, that Dr. Fat Ass. My slate is clean."

"Except for your six weeks' training at the Ministry for State Security school in Potsdam-Eiche," said Dorle. "Oh, Dorle," he said, "do you believe that if after ten years they start asking around among people who were at that time going to university in Leipzig: Did Zieger disappear in early October or not till the end of November? do you believe anyone will remember? No. As of today, everything has been told. I feel free. I could . . ."

He turned back to the piano, intending to play with both hands but then playing with only one after all. As long as Dr. Meissner has not yet passed on the supplement to his life history, he would prefer to behave according to the established cover and strum rather than play. As far as he was concerned he didn't even need to play with two hands anymore. He could always hear the other hand quite clearly as he played.

"Oh yes, Dorle," he said, "one more sentence from

today's message: All the best, Major, the Gewandhaus Orchestra is getting closer."

Wolf took the slip bearing those words out of his pocket and set fire to it.

"Not bad," he said, "a chance to play with the Gewandhaus Orchestra. Maybe Schumann, opus 54 in A Minor." He struck the chord. Dorle said: "After ten years of State Security A-3 Communications, one *single* chance to play with the Gewandhaus Orchestra!" The House of Culture in Dresden-Klotzsche would do, too, thought Wolf: but he said nothing. "And Fellbach?" asked Dorle. "I know Fellbach," said Wolf. "But not Strümpfelbach," said Dorle. "Not Strümpfelbach," said Wolf. He knelt down in front of her and laid his head in her lap. "You must leave me," he said. "I must admit it, I must advise you to." "Don't say stupid things you don't even believe yourself," said Dorle. "But then, what?" asked Wolf. Dorle shrugged her shoulders.

They went across to the bedroom. He let the shutters down with a rattle. Traffic noise became slightly fainter. Or different. It was a different noise now.

Dorle said: "This evening he was his usual self, but when he came back after seeing the minister he was really changed." "Because he got a dressing down," said Wolf. "Dr. Meissner's no problem, Dorle. He's in love with you. He'd let you know if they had anything on you. What matters most is who you're going to suggest for Brussels." Whom did he suggest, asked Dorle? If he had even the slightest interest in Sylvia, he couldn't suggest her.

24   "I know that, Wolf," said Dorle. He pressed her hand as hard as he could.

"And Fellbach, Strümpfelbach?" she asked. He said he hated responding to a private matter with the state of the world. But as long as East and West went on cheating each other ... surely one must ... enlighten. He could feel Dorle stiffen in her reaction. It was always like that. She either wouldn't or couldn't let herself be involved in any shape or form in his self-justification. He picked up the paperback from his bedside table. She nestled close to him. "Let's escape to Schiller." A theater critic had outlined the story of Schiller's play about Joan of Arc, and he had felt drawn to it. He had begun to read bits of the play aloud to Dorle. "Let's see," he began, "we're still in the prologue. Thibaut, Bertrand, Raimond go off, Joan is alone. Right?"

Dorle nodded. Wolf read without any dramatic pretensions; he was merely relaying the message to her. He was aware of becoming declamatory, yet his delivery of certain passages implied that he knew he mustn't claim this declamatory tone as applying to himself. He would then drop back and lay claim to what he was reading aloud as a reference to himself.

> Farewell ye mountains, ye beloved glades,
> Ye lone and peaceful valleys, fare ye well!
> Through you Johanna never more may stray!
> For, ay, Johanna bids you now farewell.
> Ye meads which I have watered, and ye trees
> Which I have planted, still in beauty bloom!
> Farewell ye grottos, and ye crystal springs!
> Sweet echo, vocal spirit of the vale.
> Who sang'st responsive to my simple strain,
> Johanna goes, and ne'er returns again.

Ye scenes where all my tranquil joys I knew,
Forever now I leave you far behind!
Poor foldless lambs, no shepherd now have
   you!
O'er the wide heath stray henceforth
   unconfined!
For I to danger's field, of crimson hue,
Am summoned hence another flock to find.
Such is to me the spirit's high behest;
No earthly, vain ambition fires my breast.

For who in glory did on Horeb's height
Descend to Moses in the bush of flame,
And bade him go and stand in Pharaoh's
   sight—
Who once to Israel's pious shepherd came,
And sent him forth, his champion in the fight, —
Who aye hath loved the lowly shepherd train, —
He, from these leafy boughs, thus spake to me,
"Go forth! Thou shalt on earth my witness be.

"Thou in rude armor must thy limbs invest,
A plate of steel upon thy bosom wear;
Vain earthly love may never stir thy breast,
Nor passion's sinful glow be kindled there.
Ne'er with the bride-wreath shall thy locks be
   dressed,
Nor on thy bosom bloom an infant fair;
But war's triumphant glory shall be thine;
Thy martial fame all women's shall outshine."

Noticing that Dorle had fallen asleep, he read on silently, savoring the exalted language. With its assistance
he could almost see the funny side of himself. He should

have told that Dr. Meissner even more. Everything that was innocuous. But the fellow might have thought he was trying to ingratiate himself. Well, he had to ingratiate himself. He could afford to do that. What Dr. Meissner thinks of you is really not important as long as he thinks what you want him to think. Now he takes you for the son of a veteran Communist. Who wasn't one. But who after 1945 was honored as one. With Thälmann in Buchenwald. At home his father told them that he'd been sent to a concentration camp because with his horse and wagon in Ottstedt he used to supply the camp with milk and would sometimes smuggle out mail from inmates, besides running the occasional errand. In camp his father had been made to wear the green V-stripe of a criminal rather than the red one of a political prisoner. Wolf decided to regale Dr. Meissner with further such details at the next opportunity. The file on Wolf Zieger, if it existed, could only benefit from that. Scenes from the Buttelstedt horse market perhaps, or other innocuous rustic material from Ottstedt, Berlstedt, Ballstedt, and Buttelstedt.

4

NEXT MORNING Mr. Ujfalussy came out of his front door just as Wolf reached the stairs. Side by side they walked down the steps. Mr. Ujfalussy talked loudly, rapidly, and uninterruptably. His voice was high and shrill. "You know, every time I hear you play *pi*ano (he emphasized the first syllable) I am faced with problem, why does he always play with only one hand? Why? He is *vir*tuoso, I say. I can hear that. He is using force *a*gainst himself. He has to *con*trol himself. Why, I ask myself? And ask you! If you won't tell me, I as mathematical logician will set it up as a problem, but then of course I solve the problem. Better you tell me first. Otherwise I calculate it for you. One can calculate anything, you know. Mathematics can solve all problems of whole world. During vacation in summer I have time, I calculate why Mr. Zieger play with only one hand, although he could play his Schumann *Novellettes* beautifully with two. Oh, I can see, you are afraid of my calculation! That I will include when I set up my problem. So, after vacation I know the answer. I shall tell you solution. You understand, Mr. Zieger, because I find it painful, always only one hand, I must take *revenge.*"

Laughing, he walked to his car; laughing even louder, Wolf headed for the bus stop. On the bus he sat, as always, across from a schoolgirl; on her knees was an open exercise book into which she would quickly glance and then jerk her eyes upward. She is repeating what she has just read. It makes her look as if she were in the throes of some terrible dream. And three plump little Pakistani girls were sitting in his field of vision. They had come from the Venusberg clinics. After night duty. All three of them were telling a local woman that a night nurse had cut herself on a sheet of glass, and that the cut had had to be stitched. Wolf was only listening because the three girls spoke such pure Rhenish dialect that, without looking at them, it was impossible to tell them apart from the local woman. After all, he couldn't go on thinking about Mr. Ujfalussy forever.

Just before reaching his own door, he ran into Mr. Borcherdt and Mrs. Schnellinger. Mr. Borcherdt, who was gaunt and six foot eight, was known as Tiny. He was considered a wit. And at the same time a sentimentalist. Wolf was always scared of Mr. Borcherdt, both of his witticisms and of his sentimental nature. The only thing Wolf found likable about him was the rumor that he had only been appointed to the delegation because he was the son of a regional chairman. Wolf greeted the outrageously flirting couple much more cordially than he felt, but Borcherdt said to Mrs. Schnellinger: "Ursel, he doesn't want to talk to us today."

When, at the close of the departmental meeting, Mr.

Steidle asked whether everyone was satisfied, Mr. Borcherdt groaned, so he was asked to explain himself. He gave one of his sentimental performances. No, no, he has no objections. He doesn't mind taking on the Leipzig Fair for the sixth time. By all means! What's been going on here is less of a meeting of department heads than a repeat performance. Friend Zieger, to whom the German Democratic Republic must be of the deepest concern, is allowed to escort Japanese on trips through our model *Land*, which Zieger can hardly be said to know like the back of his hand, while Borcherdt, who has had the GDR up to here, is permitted to look forward to another round with those cloned export/import comrades. Apart from the fact that friend Zieger is already in the process of preparing the participation of that model *Land* at the Moscow exhibition, so it would seem only proper for him to take his GDR brothers under his wing.

Mr. Steidle: Did Mr. Zieger see it that way, too?

Wolf sensed that the essential thing now was to remain calm, to show a minimum of reaction. Oh, said Wolf offhandedly, while listening to Mr. Borcherdt hold forth, all he had heard was the tedium that results from allowing what is supposed to be work to degenerate into routine. But perhaps Mr. Borcherdt should have considered the impact of such insinuations in the present Bonn climate, where a person is suspected of treason if he has a cousin in East Berlin. He, Wolf Zieger, refused to defend himself against such peer-spite, to justify himself before the invariably original whimsies of Mr. Borcherdt. He must ask Mr. Steidle to excuse him. And he got up, left, and went to his office, where he sat trembling at his desk.

It is impossible to fail more utterly than he had just failed. Impossible to react more atrociously than he had reacted. He was tempted to pack it in, go home and call Dorle, Come, it's all over here, everything, it's finished, off to . . . He knew that eventually he would go to Steidle and explain everything as being a side effect of an attack of gastritis. And Mr. Steidle, that kindest of men, would ask Mr. Borcherdt to join them; and Borcherdt would come, grinning, cracking jokes, he would take Wolf's hand and squeeze it until Wolf had to admit that it hurt, whereupon Borcherdt would give a deep, satisfied laugh and say that was just his Swabian heartiness, anyone who couldn't take that didn't deserve it. . . .

Wolf growled like a dog at the thought of all he would now have to put himself through, and all because for one moment he hadn't been able to control his nerves. Serves you right, he told himself. And there was nothing he was more deeply convinced of than that he totally deserved the ordeal facing him.

He rang Steidle's secretary, asked for an appointment, and imbued his voice with a beseeching undertone, from which Mrs. Lang could immediately deduce that this man Zieger was now totally dependent on her. She told him to wait. He waits, he sweats, his heart throbs in his throat. Yes, he can come now. For a few minutes. Of course only for a few minutes. On entering Mrs. Lang's office he displays the groveling gratitude that she—having been present and thus knowing how important the interview is to him—expects from him. With a knowing smile Mr. Steidle looks up from his papers and expresses his approval that Zieger has realized so promptly how wrong it was to react so humorlessly to Mr. Borcherdt's bit of fun. He, Mr. Steidle, will pass on to Mr. Borcherdt

31

that Zieger has realized his own lack of humor and is looking forward to sharing a glass of wine with Mr. Borcherdt at the "store-minders' party," which had become the favorite occasion in Bonn for clearing up such misunderstandings.

Wolf expressed his thanks fulsomely and applauded the notion of having a drink of reconciliation with Mr. Borcherdt at the store-minders' party as a marvelous inspiration.

"Yes indeed," said Mr. Steidle, "sometimes even the boss has to have a few bright ideas. Goodbye, Mr. Zieger."

Wolf, exuding humility, went to his office. Only there did he acknowledge the extent of his humiliation as he sank into his desk chair. But he was glad, too, that he had taken care of that immediately. He simply mustn't let such a thing happen to him again. When Dorle asked him that evening what kind of a day he had had, he was able to say: "All in all, not bad."

5

He couldn't have arranged to meet Sylvia in some shabby little hotel. The hotel mustn't seem like a punishment for what one did inside it. It must be able to dull the sensibilities. It must radiate some vague, higher, and hence unassailable legitimizing quality. From the concierge to the bathroom fittings. In every major city there are a few hotels capable of receiving their guests with so much approbation that each one, for as long as he remains in this hotel, is simply unable to find any fault with himself. Here he is above reproach, no matter what he does. The Senats-Hotel in Cologne just barely filled this requirement. The Dom-Hotel would probably have filled it incomparably better, but the lulling potential of that luxury class cost more per night than Wolf could regularly afford.

As far as Dorle was concerned he was in Stuttgart. That's where he would be tomorrow, too. At the Ministry of Trade and Commerce. The meeting to discuss preparations for the Baden-Württemberg industrial exhibit began at ten o'clock. Leave Cologne 5:56 A.M., arrive Stuttgart 9:51 A.M. He hoped Mr. Steidle appreciated the fact that Wolf Zieger kept an appointment in Stuttgart without spending the night there. He felt he owed it to Dorle to deceive her. Although Sylvia accepted money for the copies of the protocols, she made it seem plausible that she wasn't handing them over for the money but because she loved Wolf. She only took the money, she said, to pay the psychoanalyst her husband, Dominick, had been seeing twice a week for the past three years. Dominick was still studying for a degree in education. He was also working a bit though apparently earning very little. Counting red and white blood corpuscles was how Sylvia described Dominick's job in an institute for chemical analysis. Dominick had only started his treatment in order to get out of military service, and the longer the psychoanalysis lasted the more necessary it became. Dominick was now with his third psychoanalyst. At the moment his anxiety states were worse than ever. He had stopped taking showers because he was afraid that, when he stood under the shower, blood would come gushing out instead of water.

In Dorle's eyes Sylvia was a flirtatious, ruthless, stupid little nymphomaniac. Whenever Wolf hinted at how much Sylvia was doing to help Dominick, Dorle would give a shrill laugh. She would laugh her most insincere laugh. "Bleeding-heart stories!" she would shriek. "Of course you fall for that! I don't believe a word she says! What she does is tell everyone exactly the kind of story they'll fall for." "If she can do *that*," said Wolf, "I'll have to take lessons from her," whereupon Dorle would cry: "As if that were a problem! I can smell ten feet away what kind of story a man needs. Christ!" The word Christ exploded from her lips and seemed to end with at least five t's. Dorle knew that he picked up the protocols in Sylvia's bed, so to speak. But she would have found it unbearable to have to imagine: Now, tonight, and so on. Wolf had found a way of doctoring the facts that made them just about bearable for Dorle. A kind of affair-on-the-wing. After work and before supper, while Dominick was at the analyst's, Wolf would make a flying visit and, according to his report to Dorle, then provide sexual services that were as comical as they were agonizing and whose chief characteristic was their brevity. In any case: for the participants very unsatisfying. Dorle accepted that. Wolf admired Dorle for the strength with which she managed to bear even these doctored facts.

Wolf had left word at the hotel desk that he would be in the bar. Sylvia often turned up late. He suspected and told Dorle that besides Dominick he wasn't Sylvia's only man. Today he waited for her with genuine impatience. If she were to bring the Brussels protocol . . . that would be a triumph. And then if Dr. Bruno were to deliver Options 2 and 3, his summer was made. Actually his whole year. That meant success.

He sized up the group of men in another corner of the bar. They were celebrating something. Probably a success. They looked very successful. All between forty and fifty-seven. Did he envy them? Yes. Because they were all sitting together. Seeming to be of one mind. Were allowed to show themselves. Allowed to show off. Allowed to raise their voices. Allowed to slap one another on the back. He was a mole. Yes indeed, Mr. York. How much longer can he stand living in this illegitimate state? No, he isn't illegitimate. Not one bit. Merely illegal. But that too has to be coped with. To be in the right but unlawful. Only as concerned Dorle was he more than illegal. As concerned her he was illegitimate. And becoming more and more so. Sucked in. Sylvia had taken over—had appropriated—more and more of him. To begin with, he hadn't wanted it at all. For him it had been a relationship of expediency. But Sylvia had brought him around. That tormented him. Because Dorle trusted him. He longed for feelings he could approve of. He couldn't live permanently in a state of self-rejection. Of increasing self-rejection. Partitioned like Germany, he thought. This notion made him grin. But it was true, wasn't it? What had he been experiencing ever since being in the West? Self-rejection! More and more! He had simply let himself be talked into it, at first. At a precarious moment. After slapping Geschwendner. They were very perceptive, those comrades from the Ministry for State Security. They had heard about the incident and its consequences and deduced that he would clear out, and before he knew it they had arrived on the scene and were reminding him of what his father had fought and suffered for. So he will be performing a service for the fighting and suffering Republic. A service in the West.

The truth was that he was fleeing from defeat. He couldn't bear having witnesses. For him it was a defeat to have to give up the piano. A defeat that would never lose its devastating effect as the days and weeks went on. At the time he simply couldn't imagine that he would ever again be able to concentrate on anything. He regarded himself as incapable. Of anything. He had to get away from his silent but voraciously watching father. To work for the MfSS, and in the West, moreover: there was no better, finer solution anywhere. Not until he had crossed over to the West did he start looking for reasons for what he was supposed to do. He could see the two parts of Germany pulling apart, becoming more and more vicious toward each other. Less and less understanding, less and less sensitive, less and less aware. Informing one part about the other was called treason. On both sides. So which country was one betraying? Not Germany. . . .

Suddenly Sylvia was sitting beside him. She took a drink of his whiskey. To prevent her from dragging him up to the room right away, he beckoned the waiter. Sylvia liked mixed drinks, and she enjoyed discussing the ingredients with bartenders. Three drops of lemon juice in the martini, please, and the juice of an orange and six drops of angostura in the rum-and-gin mix. It sounded as if she lived on a diet of mixed drinks. She was wearing bib pants of pink silk. Much too conspicuous, in Wolf's opinion. She kissed him, stroked him. Her behavior was impossible. He picked up the large envelope that she had placed on the table so as to have both hands free for touching. While she was busy groping around, he put the envelope safely away in his briefcase. He could tell from the weight that it must be a sizable document.

Not because he was really interested but in order to put a damper on Sylvia, he asked how Dominick was. "Oh, Wolfy!" she said. "Teachers don't have an easy time of it. There he works himself to death and then has his essay returned by his professor with stupid remarks on it. It's scandalous the things a professor can get away with!" But at least the new analyst was an improvement. The panic fear of water had almost gone. Of course, Dominick couldn't take a shower yet, but at least he allowed himself to be touched with a wet washcloth. . . .

Wolf could listen to her with only one ear; he needed the other for the men in the opposite corner. In the increasingly loud speech of one of these men he kept hearing the word Russian. "No, no, Mr. Viehöfer," cried the voice, "that won't do, *Doctor* Viehöfer—the source of my excellent knowledge of Russian is no secret, there are in fact two versions that I can tell you about exactly, you're confusing me with Svoboda, want to bet you're confusing me with Svoboda? What do you want to bet? Come on, here are all the witnesses, you're claiming that I can't reveal where I picked up my excellent knowledge of Russian, right? That's what you're claiming, aren't you, *Doctor* Viehöfer! So come on, why don't we bet that I didn't acquire my excellent knowledge of Russian the way you may think, you see I was never a soldier, that's right, the blessing of being born late, in my case too, for the last fourteen years I've been in the USSR section of the Ministry and I've had the chance to perfect my knowledge of the country, and the language, so there you are. I've no intention of ducking the explanation you want from me, I can tell you *exactly* where I picked up my knowledge of Russian, there are two versions, you know, one official and one other, and, you know, many years ago I once stated quite openly how I picked up my excellent knowledge of Russian, and that didn't help me, not at all, because I stated quite honestly how it was, that's why I won't repeat it now, that's why there are two versions, one official and one other, but that doesn't mean that there's anything wrong with the correct version, now just wait a minute, you'll see in a moment, I'll give you both versions, that's to say it mustn't go beyond here, I'm assuming that there are no bugs here and no secret agents, just a moment, Doctor, I insist on saying it now, I have to, I was born in '31, and although I was an anti-Nazi they still put me in the *Werwolf* and threw me into the battle, most of us caught it, but not me, I went over to the Russians, and there was one fellow there who—"

At that point Dr. Viehöfer finally managed to shut him up. "Now see here, Mr. Stavenhagen, this is all quite pointless, why don't you just forget it, you can't tell me anyway where you picked up your excellent knowledge of Russian, that much is clear to each one of us, that's enough, please don't get so worked up, the main thing is, keep calm, man, we're all friends here, and how much do you expect to lose, man, if you want to bet with me let me tell you, I never bet for anything less than fifty bottles of vodka, do you want that, you can't want that, what do you mean there are two versions, now listen, Stavenhagen, just calm down, there's never more than one version of the truth, if you ask me, besides I don't even want to know, you're upsetting yourself, man, you're already upset, you're much too excited. And as for nothing going beyond here, just look around you, the fact that they're cuddling and kissing doesn't mean they can't hear, don't bother me with secrets, I don't want to hear about them, we know each other much too well. We know you didn't come by your excellent knowledge of Russian in school, and as for the rest, I suggest you keep it to yourself, understand?"

And with that he stood up, put some money down on the counter for the bartender, and left. Before he knew it, the confession-craving Mr. Stavenhagen, the oldest of the group, found himself alone. The others suddenly all had to be off, too, had engagements. Mr. Stavenhagen looked around and called: "Waiter, the bill please!" "All taken care of, sir," replied the waiter. And there was nothing to tell from his voice whether he had overheard every word of this scene or not a single one. Wolf found that admirable. There was neither scorn nor pity in that waiter's voice.

As Wolf walked past Mr. Stavenhagen he had to restrain himself from looking at the man, who was staring into space. And then maybe with sympathy, yet! He positively yanked himself and Sylvia past Mr. Stavenhagen, who appeared to be in shock: he had obviously committed an error.

In the restaurant they looked at each other like conspirators. Wolf dropped his eyes before Sylvia's gaze. He watched the young, Mexican-looking waiter, who with elegant flourishes of his spoon was preparing a mixture of pepper, salt, vinegar, oil, mustard, catsup, Worcestershire sauce, paprika, lemon juice, capers, et cetera, in the center of a plate. Next he added the ground meat, blending it thoroughly into the mixture, then pressed the new mixture through the serving fork, and finally shaped what now looked like a homogeneous mass into little patties, which he then—so that the monotonously smooth surface wouldn't be boring to the customers' eyes—proceeded to corrugate with rapid strokes of the edge of a spoon. *Bon appétit.* This high-level service, thought Wolf, is all part of the legitimizing ambience of the hotel. Everything done under such circumstances is well done. Such hotels create a moral extraterritoriality for their guests. Something he needed urgently.

When he looked at Sylvia he remembered one of Dorle's exclamations: "That woman with her bloated face!" Sylvia's face wasn't a bit bloated. Like the rest of Sylvia, her face was very fleshy. Not fat, but fleshy. She had a bit too much of everything. Her mouth always hung slightly open, as if the lips were too heavy. The eyes were too big. She was somewhat on the short side. When she lay in front of him, with her breasts reaching down over the bulges and billows of her arched torso, he felt tempted to call her "my little pygmy." And her way of speaking! Everything she said embarrassed him. But it was probably said in order to achieve the very opposite of embarrassment. She probably wanted her talk to enrapture, inspire, and daze him. For the eyes there are such things as sunglasses when the light becomes too dazzling. Something like that was needed for ears; then he might have been able to enjoy Sylvia's torrent of words. Although he was quite willing to listen to it all, he did have the feeling that such words left bruises on him or at least in him. What was he supposed to say when she told him: "You've cast a spell over me!" Or: "Since you first touched me, I live with you." Or when she phoned him in the office for no other reason than to say: "I desire you so! But I also love you. You only desire me." Or: "I can't live without you. I'm not just saying that, it's a fact." Or: "You don't know what you mean to me." Or: "My breasts are so big and they're waiting for you."

Perhaps one should call a person who advertises so

blatantly *Dirittissima*, thought Wolf. He was watching Sylvia undress in Room 302 with an equal blend of casualness and melodrama.

When she didn't speak, the atmosphere became more than usually melodramatic. As he sat down on the edge of the bed, she looked at him the way she always looked at him when he had done something wrong again. She told him at once. Using some kind of cream she had as it were deforested her lovely mound. Only at the cleft had a dark bushy fringe been allowed to remain. She had hoped, she said, that he would notice. "Have you at least fallen in love with me?" she asked. "I won't know that until I no longer have you," he said. "So then you don't know whether you love your wife," she said. I do, he thought, right now, for instance, I love my wife, and I don't have her. Because he said nothing she went on: "Do you like my vagina?" "Oh," he said, "let's hope so!" When she used clinical terms it almost gave him goose pimples. "You don't have to manipulate my clitoris, your penis does that very nicely," she said. But perhaps it wasn't even the choice of words. While their bodies were being aroused she spoke High German, almost like a schoolmarm. Maybe she simply had no luck with words. But even when she used the wrong words, she had the right feelings. Whereas he . . .

He was always glad when the time for talking was over and a more favorable means of communication got under way. Here he could keep up even less than with words, but under these circumstances he found her superior skill and variety not only not embarrassing but pleasant and more than that. Most likely she's a natural event, he thought, as she rode him remorselessly until he was reduced to a sweating, panting mare. When they lay side by side, bathed in sweat, he finally had to get around to asking her the oft-postponed question of why she continued to treat him as if he were a homosexual—was that something Dominick had introduced? She asked whether he didn't like it that way. He did, but what made her do it? Well, with Dominick she would never . . . that wouldn't seem right with him at all. What made her think it was right with Wolf? She doesn't know. She simply wants to get a little bit inside him. And that's the only place he had where she could.

After it was all over he propped an envelope between her breasts. And it stayed there. But Sylvia was offended. That wasn't how she wanted it. She was on the point of tearing up the envelope and its precious contents, and he had quickly to force her arms apart and recall her to reason. She wasn't doing it for money, she said. He knew that, said Wolf. "You're doing it for peace and all that, I'm doing it for you," she said. She told him she wouldn't open the envelope; she would place it, just as it was, in the Bible, knowing that Dominick would never go near it. She was saving up all that money for a vacation with Wolf. In Greece. On an island. In a bay.

The parting was, as always, painful. For Sylvia. And hence also for him. In whatever he was involved, he never wanted there to be any suffering. He told her that the very best thing he could think of would be to lie in bed with her until late next morning, but there was that 5:56 train . . . Sylvia's languishing sigh pursued him out of the room.

He's already paid. The all-knowing concierge lets him out and receives a tip appropriate to the ambience. As soon as Wolf is outside he hurries past the cathedral to the railway station where he just manages to catch the intercity express. As soon as he was settled in his reclining chair in the club car and had tipped his seat back, he felt equally miserable and comfortable. The briefcase containing Sylvia's big envelope was standing under his legs as they lay on the foot rest. He was tempted to read the protocol right away. Of course that wouldn't do. Luckily he was tired; he hadn't slept a wink. Sylvia would never permit that. "You can sleep at home," she would say brutally. So he dozed his way toward Stuttgart. But each time he woke up and made sure there was time to fall asleep again, he instantly became aware of the impossibility of his situation. Whenever he thought of Sylvia after they'd been together, he regretted that, when he was with her, he hadn't enjoyed being with her as much as he now wished he had enjoyed being with her. Something had prevented him from feeling 100 percent comfortable with her. Once again he had fallen short. As always. His existence was a continuous neither/nor. The person he is, is the one he is not allowed to be, and the person he's allowed to be, he isn't. So he is nobody. Living in no man's land. Now, lying back exhausted in his intercity seat, he is longing for his oriental Princess Pygmy-Belly. And that immediately triggers an even greater longing for Dorle-the-Goose. If in a polemical mood he called Sylvia "Pygmy-Belly," he was bound in all fairness to call Dorle "Dorle-the-Goose." He must be fair. I am an ethicist, he thought. His father, who had moved to central Germany after World War I, often used to say: "As an East Prussian you are an ethicist." Now his head began to shake almost uncontrollably, as in a seizure, and had he been alone in a room instead of a club car he would have shouted, louder and louder: No! No! No! No! No!

Things couldn't go on like this. Not in this way. Not in any way. The orgy of self-rejection continued to rage.

After Heidelberg he couldn't doze off again. He sat there wakeful and weary, looking out into the pitiless sunny day.

6

At 7:32 that evening he got off the train in Bonn, saw Dorle before she saw him, and also saw at once that she was in a bad state. Unlike him, she had never properly learned how to dissemble. She looked really devastated. Out of joint. One shoulder higher than the other, her head seeming to droop, her hands as if made of lead, all in all a picture of helplessness, of defeat. Whatever the reason she was about to give him for her condition, he was to blame for her standing there like that. She wasn't really standing, she was suspended. Suspended in mid-air. And he was to blame. Yet he was so looking forward to being with her. He was so happy to be coming home. All he was interested in was coming home.

Dorle's head went up. Dorle-the-Goose with her long neck on which she turned her head so jerkily. In his bureaucratic language, which made the imprecise seem exact, he thought that this was the moment when he needed feelings of which he could approve. The other travelers on the platform, in their compactness, neatness, smartness, and purposefulness suddenly seemed to him like half-people. A mass of half-people were pushing their way back and forth. Their other halves were in Leipzig, hurrying back and forth. The ones here were shining, positively sparkling in their progressiveness and positiveness. He felt attracted to all of them. How correctly they did all they were doing! But how little they were aware of themselves. They all shone with achievement, but not one of them seemed content. They don't know what they lack. And not one of them would say, if asked, that he lacked his Leipzig half, his Dresden part, his Mecklenburg extension, his Thuringian depth. They appear lost in one extreme. And the ones over there are trapped in the other. This is more divisive than that hateful stroke across the map. One should proclaim it loudly on a station platform. But he didn't have the courage. Yet he was surprised that no one shouted: We are half-people! And he most of all.

Dorle said nothing until they were in the car. Today, after everyone had left, Dr. Meissner had asked her to come to his office, and he had poured her a glass of red wine, saying that, if she would prefer, he'd take her to a café. For all he cared, he said, the entire Ministry was welcome to see him drinking a glass of wine with Dorle Zieger. For Dorle he would risk anything. Out of love. Love makes a person reckless. Did she know that? The greater the love, the greater the recklessness. Toward himself, he meant. The worst thing was to be married to a woman who not only dislikes wine but loathes it. Nothing more depressing than this lonely drinking. Downright degrading. After all, one drank in order not to feel so lonely. And then nothing makes a person more lonely than drinking. So if Dorle happened to have a problem, anything she couldn't cope with, by all means, she could talk to him anytime, about anything. And she mustn't go on calling him "Doctor" Meissner: for her he was Jürgen, after office hours anyway.

He just wanted to show her the financing plan he had worked out for her. He simply had to do something for Dorle. His mother . . . he couldn't so much as mention his mother to his wife. His mother had been an alcoholic. His mother's dentures, when the neighbors found her in the cellar, at the foot of the basement stairs, were smashed, his mother's dentures. From the fall. To make drinking more difficult for herself she had never brought up more than one bottle at a time from the cellar. So she had to make many trips down there. That was her undoing. How did Dorle like this Assmannshausen red? More than their Roussillon or not as much?

Well now, why had Dorle assigned Sylvia Wellershoff for Brussels instead of herself? He'd very much like to know. A good idea, mind you. Much as he would have liked to go to Brussels with Dorle. But he was interested in Dorle's motive. What he would like to think was that Dorle had chosen Sylvia because she was afraid that he and Dorle couldn't have ignored one another in Brussels. In the hotel. In the hotel corridor. Or couldn't have kept apart. What was the motive, Dorle? Or was it something quite different? But if so, what? Is Dorle as frank with him as he is with her? Is she? That's all he wants to know. Like he said, she can tell him everything. And he's quite sure that it's better for her to tell him everything. And he did mean everything.

At that point she had stood up, she told Wolf, picked

up the sheets with the financing plan, and thanked him for his tact and for being so extraordinarily reasonable and kind. More than that she couldn't say today. And had left the room. He had called out after her, but she had kept running until she reached the car.

Wolf said: "So?"

By this time they had arrived at their apartment. Dorle said that Meissner knew something, she was quite sure of that now. Dr. Meissner was a drowning man, said Wolf, clinging to Dorle because he could see how strong she was. After all, he said, he was doing the same thing, although he hoped he hadn't yet sunk as low as Dr. Meissner. The fellow could think of nothing beyond begetting more children, drinking Assmannshausen red, and his financing obsession. Wolf said he had grasped enough from Dorle to be able to assert that this Dr. Meissner no longer had any idea what he was working for. Maybe he was still hoping to make the jump from salary grade B6 to B7 and he might even be dreaming of B9. A horizon like that can only be veiled with alcohol, said Wolf.

"If only you were right," said Dorle. Wolf said he must remain immune to Dorle's seductive tendency to drag him with her into despair and panic. He had to do his photographing now; tomorrow was delivery day. "Oh, Wolf," said Dorle, "all day on the move and meetings and now up half the night photographing again—you're destroying yourself. And me, too," she added defiantly. "Dorle," he said, "you know that all I have is you. Apart from you, everything is coercion. If I'm destroying you, which I can't dispute, then I'm destroying myself too."

Dorle also had to report that Dieter had phoned again.

49

If next weekend they wouldn't at least look at the house he'd bought for them, he'd set fire to it. He had been shouting. Wolf drew her to him. "Say something," Dorle said. "It's almost eight thirty, and on Thursdays at eight thirty I have to receive—sorry," he said, going across to the bedroom and switching the radio to short wave: the Brahms *Lied* was already on. Later he came to her with three slips of paper and announced: "We've made it, Dorle! They're giving in. Our return home is being planned, starting today. It'll all be discussed beside the Mediterranean, in a cottage that's been booked in a vacation colony called La Côte near the small town of Istres. From July twenty-ninth to August nineteenth. Regards from the general. This means, Dorle, that MRS 903 and the Brussels protocol may have been our last big job. Now Provence, and then . . . home. Sorry. Or to Strümpfelbach. Or, after all . . . home. That's up to us. Just imagine, Dorle, only we two will decide that. You can call Dieter right away and tell him: Final decision immediately after our vacation. And on the way to Istres we'll have a look at the house in Strümpfelbach."

He put a match to the messages from Normannen-Strasse. The phone rang: Wolf picked up the receiver, held it out to Dorle, and whispered: "The Meissner pig." Dr. Meissner reported that his wife had given birth to a baby girl, who would be named Doris. "What exquisite taste," said Wolf, then went abruptly to the piano and began to hammer out the left hand of his Schumann piece. "Oh!" he exclaimed suddenly, as if in great pain. He got out his calendar. Of course. On the twenty-eighth was the store-minders' party. Of all the functions of his delegation, the party for the employees who had to spend the summer in Bonn was the most pleasant, perhaps even the most ambitious. And this time a visit from the minister in Stuttgart had been announced. The thirtieth would be the earliest they could leave, then came Fellbach, so he had to inform them at once: Cannot arrive before August second.

He told Dorle that he must run down and phone Switzerland. Dorle asked why, if he felt so secure, he didn't make his call from here? "Dorle!" he said. And was gone. Fortunately there was no Turk prancing around with the receiver this time. The Basel number answered at once. Wolf said: "Seventeen eleven twenty-one not until eight oblique two, rendezvous south." Wolf stopped off at the Akropolis bar for a quick beer: he had to flesh out this evening sortie with a bit more purpose. In case anyone was watching him. He had first walked past the phone booth, then something had occurred to him so he had turned back and made a quick call. That makes the purpose clear: his object was to go to the Akropolis.

The owner was working grimly away at the pinball machine. Normally he did this only when there weren't many customers around that early in the evening, or when he had to stay up late at night because of two or three drunks. For him to cling to the pinball machine during peak business hours could only mean that he was having a row with his family. So Wolf had to drink his beer standing beside the owner and behave as if he were interested in the stupid metal ball chasing around under the glass. The owner acknowledged his presence. At the next table the secretary of the lotto betting group was defending himself against complaints. He always selected pairs of consecutive numbers, he said, they all

51

knew that. He had once invited Wolf to join. Wolf had been bothered by the secretary's little pointed beard which, although striving to spread outward, had been pedantically trimmed like a privet hedge. "Later," Wolf had said.

Now he feels an urge to phone Dorle, Why don't you come down for a glass of beer? To take root in the Akropolis, how he would love that! But after the second beer he left. The old-age pensioner who always sat by the door called out to Wolf: "Better to drink than go down the drain."

When he got home, Dorle was lying fully dressed on the bed. He let down the shutters. This bedroom is hell. No beds could be uglier than these more-black-than-brown bulging hulks. The glass tops of the bedside tables were cracked. "I have to go to the other room," he said. She nodded. To leave her lying here like this—one shouldn't be capable of doing that. But the protocol had to be photographed before the night was over.

The next evening they had tickets for a concert. It was a favorite habit of his—although he would smile at it himself—to save time by combining two or more engagements. After the concert he first took Dorle to their car in the underground garage, then went to the ticket automat. He was the last in line. When it was his turn, another man arrived who, when Wolf was about to turn away, called out: "Would you have change for a fifty?" Wolf replied: "Maybe." The other man said: "That would be a big help." Wolf said: "I'll have a look. How d'you want it broken down?" "As small as possible." Whereupon Wolf took the fifty-mark bill and handed over the film and five ten-mark bills. When Wolf returned, Dorle was sitting in the car crying bitterly. She apologized at once. He knew why she was crying. He could have kicked himself at the concert when the soprano was singing "Close to my heart, close to my breast," from Schumann's *Frauenliebe und Leben* cycle:

> Only a woman, babe at breast,
> Drinking its fill, by her caress'd;
> Only a mother, she alone
> Can call true love and bliss her own.
> Oh, how my heart aches for the man!
> Know bliss like this he never can.

He had just managed to stop himself from giving Dorle's hand an understanding squeeze. That would have made the aptness even more obvious. But what was there left now that couldn't be interpreted as either allusion or threat? They had apparently reached an impasse. Most singers are unintelligible, but tonight that full, round voice had clearly enunciated every single word of the song.

When they entered the bedroom he again had the notion that this was hell. The traffic noise, the cramped space, the cheap, shabby furniture, the ghastly flowered wallpaper. Since they hadn't intended to settle here they had furnished the place in a makeshift way, with the idea of spending as little money as possible on this temporary accommodation. Now they had been living for nine years in this squalid temporary state. Their life was seeping away in these dilapidated makeshift surroundings. If at least he could talk to Dorle about what mattered most: his increasing self-rejection! He had become impossible. Without Dorle's approval he was impossible. He was positively disintegrating without her sanction. He must at least, somehow, make her aware of the hapless state he was in and could not mention.

When they were in bed he picked up the thin yellow paperback. Dorle immediately snuggled up to him. Whenever he read aloud, she wanted to be as close to him as possible. He started off again in a purely informational tone, but then involuntarily became more dramatic while making sure that the most important part, the burden of the text, was not drowned in rapture. And once again—and he knew that only he could enjoy this— he enjoyed the way this text absorbed his personal problem into a comedy that sprang from melodrama. He said: *"Maid of Orleans,* Act IV."

> *A hall adorned as for a festival. Joan alone.*
> Why was I doomed to look into his eyes!
> To mark his noble features! With that glance,
> Thy crime, thy woe commenced. Unhappy
>   one!
> A sightless instrument thy God demands,
> Blindly thou must accomplish his behest!
> When thou didst see, God's shield
>   abandoned thee,
> And the dire snares of hell around thee
>   pressed!

He read until Dorle had fallen asleep. It would have been impossible for him to stop any earlier. He wanted to avoid having to discuss the relevance of the Schiller text to his own case. But he did want to read her the text. He was willing to risk Dorle discovering the relevance. That she had fallen asleep reassured him; but it also worried him. He wanted to get out of this no man's land. Now Dorle was lying beside him, and each time he looked at her he felt a sharper stab of pain. There was nothing so unmistakable as this pain.

What nonsense to keep using the word illegitimate. It was simply this pain. Or, to be more exact, this ache.

7

WHEN CONFRONTED BY the unresolved, one must try to sidestep it. As soon as they were driving along French roads, Dorle cheered up. She had always been a champion of France, always carried on the battle about their future direction by enlisting the help of France. There was nothing she didn't resort to now. Without this light she would become depressed. As they drove through the rolling Burgundian countryside: "I'd really miss this!" As soon as they turned off the freeway in Provence she acted as if they had narrowly escaped a danger. When plane trees lined the road, she said: "Why don't we move to France?" Implying: instead of East Germany. She pointed to the fields between walls of cypresses and to the fields between walls of bamboo, exclaiming: "Look, oh do look!" Should he say: Ottstedt, Berlstedt, Ballstedt, and Buttelstedt can also ... ? No, he could say nothing. "Stop a moment!" she cried, and got out. "Why don't you get out, too?" she cried. "Oh, the smell! Whatever you take hold of here is spicy! Look, there's a special avenue leading to each house in its field!"

In Saint-Rémy people were dancing between the tables in broad daylight. "They're alive," Dorle said. They had to stop because Dorle wanted to see whether a yapping poodle would succeed in tearing his master away from a conversation he was having with a woman outside her garden gate. The man says goodbye, the woman goes back into her garden, and the iron gate is closed, but their conversation continues. Dorle understands French. All that Wolf keeps hearing is: *Alors moi je....*

Dorle has the map on her knees and navigates him to Istres and through Istres to the vacation colony of La Côte. A steep slope, thinly forested, where their cottage was; below it, the lagoon. The *patron*, a Dutchman, his young wife, a Tunisian, a kind of advertisement for Mediterranean eroticism. There was a letter for Wolf. After they had moved into their cottage and were lying on their lounge chairs on the terrace, he said: "How d'you like this?" "Open the letter," she said. The letter gave directions for finding the villa in Sainte-Maxime. On Friday. The writer was looking forward to seeing them. They were to count on two days. And they were to be prepared for a surprise.

Wolf assumed there was someone there from the East; maybe even Comrade Bergmann, whom he had never met personally. For over five years he had been getting his assignments from Bergmann; now at last he was going to meet him. "If we don't like it there," said Wolf, "we'll drive back the same evening, that's understood. But it won't hurt us to drive there. Côte d'Azur, Dorle!" "Vacation," said Dorle. "You bet!" said Wolf. He reached out to Dorle. "The fact that *they* have sent us here— somehow that bothers me," she said. "We're supposed to be on vacation, aren't we?" "We *are* on vacation,

Dorle," he said, "until we understand cicadas better than people." Dorle said: "Promise." "I swear it," said Wolf. "I'd rather you promised," said Dorle. And they lay back again. *Les cigales ne commencent pas avant neuf heures,* said Dorle. He asked for a translation.

Next morning Dorle announced that they would not be swimming in this water, Etang de Berre. "Those people have maneuvered us to an industrial sump," she says. Dorle asks the way to the sea, to a beach. About forty kilometers. Through Istres, to Fos-sur-Mer, through an industrial zone with intimidating giant structures, to Port de Fos and finally to the beach named after Napoleon. A city of huts, tents, recreational vehicles. But at some point it opened up, with fewer people, with only one family every thirty meters. This was the domain of the fishermen. Always there was a man tending his seven fishing rods stuck at an angle in the sand. Always a woman squatting on the sand, resting her head in her hands. Always two children digging in the sand as if in a dream. This is the domain of the mistral, the biting north wind that drives the sand in sharp jets against every unprotected particle of skin, tears at the crests of the waves pushing against it from the sea, sprays the spume toward the sea. The men walking from one fishing rod to the next savor the pressure of the mistral with every step they take. Dorle and Wolf dug themselves a good-sized hollow against this wind in the shelter of their car.

"It's wonderful here," Wolf said. "Here, yes," said Dorle. "No one will find us here," said Wolf. For that she kissed him. "Here's where we'll stay, forever," she said. "I'll open up a fried fish stand back there in the tent city."

58

That evening Dorle insisted they go to the Cour de Nuit. In Istres. She had seen a poster. Wolf would much rather have stayed on their terrace, with red wine and the sound of the cicadas. For here he too was drinking wine. And not only to please Dorle. Dorle knew the way, the parking lot, a crêperie, and then the arena. Dorle looked on like a child. He looked at Dorle more than at the arena. Three clowns, a young black bull. The clowns tease the bull but don't hurt it. The bull gallops, full of taurine rage, toward the clowns, who escape every genuine danger by parodying the movements of a matador. Then it's the turn of the young boys. Ages ten to twenty. They're supposed to rob the bull of a cockade. An announcer explains this; Dorle translates it for Wolf. The longer it takes, the more the local firms jack up the prize money. Now a fourteen-year-old starts running. He has calculated the route of the bull that has started ahead of him, races off, cuts across the bull's path right in front of its nose, and snatches a cockade from the bull's head as he dashes past. Loud applause. When he tries to get the second cockade by the same method, the bull catches him by the sweater, but he just has time to leap over the arena's protective fence.

Dorle didn't have her fill until the program was really over and spectators were streaming from all sides onto the arena to prolong the evening in a public festival. For a while she even wanted to stay and watch that too: only when Wolf said he was thirsty could she actually tear herself away. They drove home and lay down again on the lounge chairs on their terrace. "That boy," said Wolf, "he couldn't have been more than fourteen—as soon as he sees the bull starting he runs off, runs as fast as he can and cuts across the bull's path only inches from its

59

horns, and snatches the cockade from its head as he dashes past. If he had miscalculated he couldn't possibly have stopped himself. He simply risked everything." "For a hundred-franc cockade," said Dorle. She had liked the clowns better; she could do without potential disaster. She meant it. *Santé!*

"When he went after the second cockade," said Wolf, "he was no longer risking everything, and that was enough for things to go wrong. You have to race off and know it'll work, then it works. If you play safe you'll never make it."

"The clowns," said Dorle, "they were good. With their matador parodies. Everything should only be parodied." In her opinion. *Santé.* Potential disaster should be abolished.

"We're trying to prevent it, Dorle," said Wolf.

"*You* are," said Dorle.

"You and I," said Wolf, "by means of parody. That's all it is, what we're doing between these two wrong-headed halves of Germany."

In the middle of the night Wolf was roused by the clink of metal on metal. His body immediately stiffened with fright. Then he heard whispering, French. The bed was right beside the open window; anyone could have vaulted into the room from the outside. Gradually he recovered from his fright. He woke Dorle. Dorle listened to the whispering, then said: "I think they're changing a tire." Wolf crept to the window. She was right: illuminated by a lantern placed on the ground, a naked torso, one man in trousers, the other in shorts—they were changing a wheel. Inside the car sat a woman; the most visible object through the open door was a knee. Wolf quietly groped his way back into bed. He didn't want them to know they were being observed.

On Friday the drive via Marseilles and Toulon to Sainte-Maxime. As soon as they were on the Côte d'Azur highway, everything changed. They were driving through an overcrowded garden. No more mistral. No wide horizon. An overpopulated grandeur, a motionless heat. More cars than people. All the drivers here seemed to have resigned themselves to being in excess as they carefully and patiently wound their way around one another, waiting until the approaching car had squeezed by. It was as if they had all abandoned hope of ever moving forward.

Right from the start Dorle had opposed this drive with gloomy suspicion, with wordless disapproval. This time it was Wolf who pointed out incredible trees and spectacular villas and breathtaking views of bays and ocean. Did she really want to run everything down merely because she disapproved of their objective? At Le Lavandou he managed to find a space where he could squeeze in his compact. Perhaps Dorle's mood could be changed by a swim. Although the bay was as overcrowded as everything else along here, there was room to swim in the calm, deeply transparent water. No sooner had they tried to swim out into less populated water than a huge motorboat came speeding toward them, in it a father shouting away at his daughter. She was standing topless at the wheel and apparently being taught how to approach the shore from the sea without killing more swimmers than necessary. Wolf longed for the limitless stretch of sand of the Plage Napoléon at the mouth of the Rhône. Even out here in the water the air was saturated with the reek of suntan lotions steaming up from thousands or tens of thousands of bodies. They gave up; drove on.

Wolf had memorized the route sufficiently to find his way to Villa Ma Joie without Dorle's help. But eventually he did need Dorle. She had to ring the bell, speak into the intercom, and announce in French that the Ziegers had arrived. The gate opened, and they drove through to the main building, where they were indeed received by Comrade Bergmann. Wolf pressed the strong hand as firmly as he could; he was feeling shaky, all limp inside. A handsome type, brownish blond, thick hair ending in a peak on his forehead, brownish gold mustache, musical nose—Wolf's term for aquiline noses—brown eyes, cheerful expression; in any event, extremely pleasant and affable. The handshake signaled: he was the stronger of the two, no question. It was almost like shaking hands with Tiny Borcherdt. And then Bergmann drew Wolf into an embrace. Kisses left and right, East European style. Presumably Wolf was expected to do likewise with Bergmann's secretary, Marga Haubold. He couldn't bring himself to, not that quickly. And upstairs in the terrace room—this was probably the promised surprise, and it really was one—the general.

On being told this by Bergmann as they entered the room, Wolf adjusted promptly enough to be able to stand at attention before the Comrade General and say: "Seventeen eleven twenty-one, York, reporting as ordered."

"Comrade Major!" cried the general. "This is indeed a pleasure! Welcome! Welcome!" Another genial type, Wolf thought. Wonderful. And the young woman: Sonya, the general's wife. Wolf's immediate thought was: wife number which? But she was friendly, too, and relaxed, obviously delighted by the visit. Dispensing with formality she gave Dorle an affectionate hug. That made Wolf feel good. An elderly caretaker couple: Marius and Thérèse. And coffee and cakes were served immediately. The general praised the French-roasted coffee. His hair grew in the same kind of peak as Comrade Bergmann's, only it was not as thick, and it was darker, flecked with gray. And his nose was even larger, even more aquiline. A fleshy arch of a nose above flabby, no longer symmetrical lips; the upper lip curved up slightly on the right. Perhaps because for years the general had been turning an intended remark into a smile. Wolf would have taken the general for a Frenchman rather than a Berliner.

The general expressed surprise that the French method of roasting coffee did not extend beyond the border. In West Germany, he said, the coffee was no better than in the GDR, whereas in Switzerland it was almost as good as in France. Bergmann maintained that there were several kinds of coffee in Moscow, and that in Georgia and Armenia the coffee was even better than here. No one contradicted him.

The general announced the program: the ladies will be driven into town for some leisurely shopping; the men will talk business, in the evening there will be a formal dinner. Bergmann added: The Ziegers shouldn't set any limits to their expectations, Comrades Thérèse and Marius were masters of their profession. He must say that even in Tbilisi and Yerevan he hadn't eaten much better than here at Ma Joie, and that was saying something. After dinner the festivities would continue, said the general. He had to apologize for allotting a greater role to entertainment than was really appropriate to a Yavka, for he felt he must now confess to the Ziegers that they had Sonya, too, to thank for this Yavka—not Sonya alone, but also Sonya. The thing was, they had been married six weeks ago, and Sonya had been allowed to choose where they should go for their honeymoon. As a member of the spoiled generation, Sonya had opted for the capitalist world. And who has the best connections with the capitalist world? The Poles, of course. That's how they got here. Ma Joie had once belonged to Maciej Sczepanski, that quintessence of Polish corruption: if it had still belonged to him the general would never have set foot in it. But it now belonged to the people again.

Soon they were standing on the terrace waving to the women, who were being driven into town by a French chauffeur. Bergmann was the first to stop waving. The general remained standing even after the car had disappeared, as if he couldn't tear himself away from the view of town and sea. Bergmann said that he personally was inclined to favor the Crimea. The Black Sea in general. Here everything was so terribly built up, wasn't it? For him it had come almost as a shock to see how completely they had done away with nature. He gave Wolf a challenging look. "Don't ask me, Comrade Bergmann—I was never in the Crimea." Bergmann: "I can only say, it'll be an eye-opener for you." The general said he would take a little nap.

In a room on the second floor the working papers lay ready and waiting. Bergmann explained what the Ministry for State Security expected of Wolf before he would be allowed to return home. It was all tied in with the camouflage technology of the "Stealth" project. From the titanium nitrate hardening of the wings to the computer responsible for correcting route phases. Wolf was disappointed. He hadn't expected that much work. Bergmann was not sparing with his praise. The final options of MRS 903 had arrived, which meant a great step forward in the ECM technology. After they had sat down, Bergmann prepared to speak for the record. He asked Wolf whether he had any objection to their conversation being taped. Wolf had to laugh: of course he had no objection. Bergmann said that way it would be easier to make the most of this afternoon's work.

Seeing Wolf's disappointment, Bergmann told him that during the past year enemy reconnaissance had yielded information for East Germany to the value of some 550 million marks. The cost had been five million. There was no enterprise in the state that could rival the People-Owned Production Unit "Listen and Look." Wolf had contributed to that. To a most significant degree. Wolf demurred. What disappointed him, he said, was that this new assignment program did not provide for a firm date for his return home. But he needed a firm date. One on which he could really plan. For years he had been putting off his wife. She was thirty-five and wanted a child. And so did he. Comrade Bergmann said: "We are at war. Imperialism is holding a knife to our throat. They want to wipe us off the face of the earth. For them, the earth would quite simply be a better place if there were no socialist states on it. They want to arm us to death. They won't give up until we build so many cannons that we can't produce any more potatoes. Coexistence—an illusion. Here—we've brought this along for you: *Silent Front*. By your colleague Ivan Vinarov . . ."

"You don't have to lecture to me, Comrade Bergmann," said Wolf.

Bergmann said: "You're bringing your wife into this,

Comrade Zieger! That means your 'enemy image' is becoming blurred. Not that you're aware of that yourself, of course. I can hear it in every word you've been saying. That's all I do hear. Capitalism is more successful than we are. You're finding that out. But what you haven't found out is that it is more successful because it appeals to the baser human instincts. That pays off. Only in the field of enemy reconnaissance are we superior. So far. Because we are better motivated. And that's precisely what you are jeopardizing when you give the *petit bourgeois* family idyll priority over what the worker-and-peasant state is demanding from you at a critical moment."

Bergmann did not speak forcefully. He used a very calm, that's-the-way-it-is tone. He opened up insights. He didn't agitate. Certainly not in his tone of voice.

Wolf said he felt that at the moment they were living in peace, although a shaky peace. He was doing this work solely for this peace, to render it more reliable.

"And for the future of Communism," Bergmann added in his wonderfully deep, masculine voice. Just so Wolf didn't entirely forget that!

"But peace is beyond discussion," said Wolf.

"Do you really want us to get into the peace debate," said Bergmann, "now?"

"I only want to say," replied Wolf, "that I wouldn't kill. For anything or anybody. In the days when they were still working with the prussic acid pistol, I wouldn't have been available. What I was really trying to explain was that my wife can't wait forever. And that nothing is worth a further postponement." Bergmann said he would like to suggest that he have a quiet talk with Wolf's wife, just the two of them, where the most private matters can be brought up just as much as political issues, an embedding of individual destiny in the context of what socialism can and cannot demand of us and why it can do that ... so really, Comrade Zieger could regard this problem as solved.

The general entered. Bergmann went on talking, his tone never gaining in force or rhetoric but remaining one of profound affability. Needless to say, they have trained a future replacement whom they can activate at any time. But he felt it would be premature to start him off right now, and especially on such a big job as "Stealth." He would break under the strain and become useless to them. But so be it, if it comes to that. If Zieger forces their hand. If he decides to quit on them. They wouldn't care for that much. Naturally. They demand of each person what they demand of themselves: the utmost. There can be no other way.

"The utmost," said Wolf. "Hmm."

"Tell you what," said Bergmann, "I'll pop over and see you both."

The general said: "Say Yes, Comrade Zieger. I have to go to Marseilles anyway the day after tomorrow—he can drop me there, it's not that far from Marseilles to your place."

"While Comrade General is watching his soccer game," Bergmann said, "I'll take your wife for a cup of coffee. In Istres."

"Racing Club Paris versus Olympique Marseille," said the general. He wouldn't want to miss that.

Bergmann said that Dynamo Berlin versus Dynamo Dresden would be his preference.

"Don't be so chauvinistic, Comrade," said the general.

67

"Racing Club Paris have Litbarski on their team, Wolf must have already seen him—he played for years in Cologne."

Wolf confessed that he had no time for soccer. "What with all that Schumann," said the general. "With all that Schumann," repeated Wolf, trying to sound as if he were saying: That's what you think. The general ignored this and said: "There's a time for everything." Bergmann said: "In any case, the Gewandhaus Orchestra is coming closer." Incidentally, he had brought along something else, a rather unusual little thing, especially for Zieger's wife—she would like it. Zieger could also regard it as a kind of lifebelt. In case anything should go wrong. They would simply play this tape to Dr. Jürgen Meissner, the ministerial director—and he swore that Dr. Meissner would obey the Ziegers like the best-trained little dog. As they were aware, the ministerial director had recently buried his mother in Jena, a lady who had been fonder of alcohol than of people. And the son had taken the opportunity for a side trip to the most depraved part of Leipzig, and, instead of grieving, what did they think he'd done in Room 402 in the Astoria Hotel—it had to be heard to be believed! Perhaps because Wolf didn't jump at it, he added: "We're doing our best to make things a bit easier for you people on the invisible front." Wolf was reminded of Dr. Meissner's complaint about the vanished terry cloth in East Germany. The general said it was time to wind things up. When Bergmann shook his head doubtfully, the general told them that at a recent meeting of functionaries someone had remarked: "Comrades, wherever we are, nothing works. But we can't be everywhere." The general laughed; Bergmann smirked.

When the women returned, Wolf saw at once that the expedition had turned out a disaster—although only for Dorle. She looked almost lifeless. Her features seemed frozen, numb. Sonya, on the other hand, chattered away excitedly about all the wonderful things she had seen and bought. Marga Haubold smiled knowingly, or condescendingly: anyway she seemed to have understanding for Sonya's garrulousness, whereas Dorle's expression was anything but appropriate to Sonya's prattling recital. Fortunately it was time to get ready for dinner.

While they were changing, Wolf asked what had happened. Dorle asked what was supposed to have happened. She volunteered no information but remained in low spirits. At dinner the general had praise for Sczepanski's wines, saying it spoke against the perfectability of the world that a pig like Sczepanski should have such good taste. And would Comrade Bergmann kindly refrain from repeating that he had drunk infinitely better wine in Georgia? "What's that fellow Sczepanski doing now?" asked Wolf. Bergmann replied that Sczepanski, being Polish, had been Catholic and hence doubtless opposed to cremation so was probably rotting quietly away in some Polish cemetery. "He was executed," said the general. "And in Poland," Bergmann added. Sonya asked whether they couldn't talk about less gruesome things. "Show some consideration for a mother-to-be, Comrades," she said. She was just dying to rush back to her room and plunge her hands into all those marvelous little pink and blue baby things! "That's right, Comrade Father, I've bought pink *and* blue. What I don't need, my sister can have. She's in the family way, too, you see. I must say, Doris, without you I couldn't have managed. It seems that Russian isn't a world language after all! But

Doris wouldn't give up till we found ourselves right in the center of baby heaven. The lengths the French go to to dress up their newborns! I must say, if that had any effect on a people's self-esteem, our people would be way behind. . . ."

Wolf now realized why Dorle was depressed. He tried to interrupt Sonya. Dorle can't be enjoying this topic. "I must say," he interjected into Sonya's flow, "Marius and Thérèse are past masters in that most delicate of all areas—fish." As an avid cook he'd appreciate an explanation of how something appearing so charmingly on the menu as *Loup de mer grillé au fenouil* was prepared. But Sonya immediately drew all eyes and ears back to herself. "André!" she shrieked. "Oh André!" Got up and ran outside. The general rushed after her. "Sonyasha!" he called, "what is it?" Bergmann said: "Don't worry. Sonya's autonomic nervous system is highly unstable at the moment." Which was only to be expected during the first three months. He was quite sure it was nothing serious. Just then the general and his wife came back; with two fingers Sonya was holding up a ring. She had thought she'd lost it or left it somewhere in town, but luckily she hadn't. The general explained that Sonya couldn't bear the thought of losing this particular ring because it had been his first gift to her. He had brought it back from Moscow for her. "But it's beautiful, too, not just from Moscow," said Sonya, now displaying the ring on her hand. "Amethyst," she said. She just loved this pointed oval. Wolf was tempted to say that fortunately Dorle hadn't lost her turquoise, set in ten-carat gold and bought in New York. But from every point of view that would have been a mistake. So the general's first name was André. He really did look as if he had some French ancestors.

After dinner they moved to the salon, where Cognac, red wine, and liqueurs were served. "This Cointreau could make me quite ruthless toward that unborn life," said Sonya. Luckily the general still had to take care of a few points on the agenda. "The high points of our Yavka!" he said. And there was Marius, asking Wolf to follow him into the next room where he opened a suitcase containing a new uniform. National People's Army. Rank of major. In garbled French and German, Marius indicated that Comrade Captain was to try it on. It was a perfect fit.

Wolf came back, saluted, but, on seeing the horror in Dorle's eyes, turned his military bearing into something deliberately awkward, clumsy. Obviously he couldn't afford to appear too clownish, he realized that. Bergmann and the general congratulated him effusively. Bergmann wished him much joy and an equal amount of success in the interest of the cause. "Now the highest point of all!" said the general. "Comrade Haubold!" And she was already opening the little case, from which the general lifted a decoration. "Comrade Major," he said, "in the name of the chairman of the State Council, and in view of your many years of tireless, circumspect, courageous, and successful service as a scout on the invisible front, it is my privilege to award you the Fatherland's Distinguished Service Order in Gold."

He pinned the decoration to Wolf's chest. They all congratulated him. Wolf expressed his thanks. "There now," said the general, "that really was the final and culminating point of the agenda. That's the end of the

71

official part. Comrade Major, this afternoon you were a bit inclined to make fun of your old general—who doesn't feel that old, thanks to Sonya—for wanting to watch Olympique Marseille versus Racing Club Paris the day after tomorrow. My response was: there's a time for everything. Now it's your turn. Marius!"

Marius opened the double doors and ushered them into a music room containing a grand piano. Open. Wolf was instantly attracted by the instrument. By the music on the stand. "Schumann!" he cried. "Dorle! Schumann's *Novellettes!*"

His voice broke. He was in tears. He was sorry about that. He apologized. He was going slightly crazy, he said; dreadful, he thought to himself. Another five seconds, and he'd be himself again.

The general said that it had been noted with pained regret, via A-3 Communications, that Comrade Scout, in order to eliminate even the slightest possibility of damage to his cover, had suppressed his greatest passion—playing the piano—or at least had restricted it to practicing with one hand. As they knew, before going to the invisible front our major had studied the piano for a year, at the music academy in Leipzig. "So now, my dear Wolf, it's all yours, here at last is a chance for us to hear our Schumann!" Everyone was seated. Wolf sat down at the piano, looked at the music. Instinctively he began with his left hand. "Both hands!" cried Sonya.

Wolf nodded, then looked at his audience. Shook his head like someone who still can't believe that it's possible to be so pleasantly surprised. It was some time before he found himself able to play with both hands, then he plunged into it. He found it incredibly difficult, but he was determined to do it. So he played, although not for long. Then he stopped, shook his head again. This time, however, without strength, without tension, without hope. He picked up the music from the stand, closed the piano, and joined the others.

"It's no use," he said. "I'm sorry. But never mind. That really was the most marvelous, most fantastic surprise I've had for . . . for a long time. Thank you, Comrade General. That was more . . . than the decoration. But, please, now . . . let's have another drink. There's a time for everything. Not for Schumann now, I'm positive. When I get back. Over there. Home. Then. Not now. I'm sorry. Let's go back to the other room. Please."

8

THEY WERE GLAD to be back again, in their own surroundings, at the Plage Napoléon, also overcrowded but in quite a different way. The hodgepodge of huts, tents, and recreational vehicles was absorbed into an inviolable expanse; there still remained an enormous space. The sandy beach stretching away to infinity, where everything petered out. The mistral in which the fishing rods bent over. No one can actually talk in the mistral. Not only do the sea and the wind prevent you from hearing each other but you are much too dazed. Once again Dorle became a different person when she was back with her ordinary folks and all their kids and dogs and fishing rods. The industrial silhouettes of USINE D'ACIERS, MINÉRALIERS, and AIR LIQUIDE outlined against the landward horizon now seemed almost protective. Suntan lotions could not defile the air here. In retrospect Wolf agreed with Comrade Bergmann: on the Côte d'Azur the hotels had taken over. Perhaps over here the industrial monsters had scared off the hotels. In any event, thus pondering, he drove past the glittering behemoths with somewhat more friendly feelings than the first time.

After they had more or less dug themselves in again, Dorle talked into the mistral. Perhaps the idea of not being heard made it easier for her to speak. She had no doubts whatever, she said, that the people at Villa Ma Joie were kind and helpful. She really reproached herself for having been so uptight. Prejudiced, nervous, and completely self-centered: that's what she had been. That would haunt her for a long time. For her, the whole bunch had been a troop sent out to bring back Wolf. "On the contrary," said Wolf. Oh, sure, but basically their job was to tie him down. Their orders had been to prove that he belonged over there. That's why she had been so sensitive to whatever they said. That Sonya, who was of course totally relaxed, enviably relaxed, in fact, but then during their shopping trip to Sainte-Maxime she mentions at least five times how incredible she finds it that she and her husband have been allowed to travel to the CW together. What a proof of trust toward her husband and herself! After all, they have no children over there, so there's nothing to stop them from staying in the CW. Dorle had had to ask what that meant, the CW. "Do you know?"

"The capitalist world, of course," Wolf told her.

He should have taught her the basic vocabulary of those people in advance, said Dorle. No kids means no hostages over there, yet they've been allowed to travel to the CW! Didn't he think that was terrible? Did he think it was really so incredible, as Sonya claimed, that their government should rely on her returning together with her husband? And they will return! What's more, voluntarily! That's what *she* finds really incredible! They go back voluntarily to where they belong. Whoever would say such a thing here! A Dutchman, an Englishman? They don't find it incredible that they are allowed to leave and go home again, do they! Then that Sonya practically goes overboard when she plunges her hands into those baby things! At that point she was fully counting on sympathy: evidently there are no baby things over there that can send an expectant mother into a frenzy. If Comrade Haubold hadn't intervened, Sonya would have thrown all her money away on baby things.

Wolf said: "Now don't you start holding forth about consumerism, Dorle." Dorle said she had no intention of condemning anything or anybody, she simply found it sickening when baby things became that important. Wolf was glad Dorle hadn't heard what Bergmann had said about Wolf's "enemy image." He said he found it incredible that Dorle should have refused to have a talk with Bergmann, who obviously had never had anything of the kind happen to him before. Bergmann had been quite embarrassed in his surprise. But surely there was nothing she could say against the general, was there? She wasn't saying anything against Bergmann either, said Dorle, she felt thoroughly sorry for him. Why, she didn't know. Perhaps it was presumptuous on her part. When she looked at Bergmann she felt like bursting into tears: he seemed so pathetic to her. "But the general!" Wolf said again, "the general, you must agree!" Dorle said nothing. Wolf went on: "In his position, Dorle. Just look at those stuffed shirts holding similar positions in Bonn. A bunch of smoothies. But the general—I could work with him, I know that."

"What's a 'yavka' anyway?" asked Dorle. "A rendez-vous," said Wolf, "a conspiratorial meeting." What she really found disgusting, said Dorle, was the Meissner tape. Imagine setting a trap like that for someone who's just on a visit! Dis-gus-ting! "But quite normal," said Wolf, "everywhere." She doesn't believe it. She simply doesn't believe it.

Wolf inserted the cassette into the set. The Schumann piano concerto. Wind and sea didn't leave much of Schumann. But a mistral-shredded Schumann seemed more appropriate now than a pure concert-hall version. They lay close together. Wolf more in her arms than she in his.

The following day to Avignon. It was Dorle who couldn't pass by any famous town without taking in the sights. What if they ever had children, she said, and they were to tell them they had been in this area but not in Avignon!

So Wolf followed Dorle's unrelenting footsteps and dissertations through the historic labyrinth. Dorle could absorb experiences much better than he could, he knew that. Especially sights. He could hear more than he could see. But he enjoyed being guided by Dorle through these walls that preserved every footstep from the past. In the late afternoon, when Wolf's back was hurting even more than his feet, they emerged through a low archway onto a tiny, ancient square. Ahead of them walked a black woman of about twenty-two, pressed close against a white woman of about twenty-eight. The white woman was leading a long, low-slung dog on a wide, white leash of shiny patent leather. Apparently the intimacy of the square suddenly got to the black woman; she yanked the white woman still closer to her. They were both wearing skin-tight denim shorts and white blouses. The white woman almost fell over backward from the black woman's sudden jerk. But that was what the black woman wanted. She catches the heavier white woman on her right arm, then lets the protective arm sink down the white woman's back and thrusts her hand from behind into the denim crotch and pokes around in it. Almost instantly the white woman loses all self-control. Her right hand can no longer hold the leash. The dog stops, stays behind, the two women stagger about. Wolf and Dorle look on in fascination.

Wolf said very softly: "I think I'll give myself up." A clock striking six muffled the last words.

Dorle said: "What did you say?"

"Come on," said Wolf.

He pulled her firmly forward, past the couple, out of the square.

9

On the drive home they stayed away as long as possible from the freeway because Dorle wanted to see more villages and take along a few bottles of wine. And so they found themselves in Gigondas. Suddenly Dorle exclaimed: "Stop a moment!" In the window of a store that seemed to contain everything, she had seen a platter. Wolf found a parking spot, and they walked back. Dorle hadn't been mistaken. The platter was beautiful. Handpainted. "It'll probably be too expensive," Dorle said. The motherly woman inside said: "Four hundred and fifty francs." They could just afford that.

Then they drove on, looking for a truly charming place to spend their last night in France. Dorle insisted that they must be able to have dinner in the garden. Wolf insisted on a bedroom that, rather than discourage you the moment you walk in, gives you a little thrill of pleasure. They drank wine from the Rhône. Dorle drank much faster than Wolf. She led the conversation. She was so happy, she said, to have found that platter. Just imagine, rack of lamb *provençale* on that platter. "For Dr. Meissner," said Wolf. "For you, for me, for our . . . family," said Dorle. "It's a platter for a family, Wolf." "Yes, Dorle," he said. "Don't worry," she said, "I'm not going to bring up the subject of children again. But family—surely I can say that—family—can't I? Aren't we a family then? Of course we are! You and I are a family, aren't we?"

"And a great one," said Wolf.

"Here's to you, Wolf," said Dorle, "my dear, dear Wolf!"

"Here's to you, Dorle!" said Wolf.

"I'm sorry," said Dorle.

He was the one to apologize, said Wolf.

"No, no, no," she cried, in a loud, almost harsh voice. "If anyone has to apologize, it's me, me!"

Wolf said: "Please, Dorle!"

"Now you just listen to me!" cried Dorle, who either didn't count on anyone there understanding German or didn't care. "You must forgive me for always picking on you whenever you've been involved with women. That won't happen again. That lack of trust is over and done with, I can tell you that. It was petty of me. You're doing something for a greater cause, and I pick on you like the worst kind of shrew. I know you like me." And silently she mouthed the words "love me." "As I do you," she said. "I've discovered that on this vacation. That's why I'm apologizing. Regardless of what you have to do in this business . . . I simply trust you now. Not that I have a choice anyway. Here's to you, boyo. To total trust."

"Oh, Dorle, Dorle, Dorle," said Wolf. "Here's to you!"

He had to get her off this subject. But how? Although

she had been drinking too fast, her mind was wide awake; she would notice any attempt to force her out of her mood and cling to it all the more stubbornly.

Things didn't really need to get any better, she said. She'd be satisfied if they stayed the way they were.

"They'll get even better," he said softly.

"Please!" she protested. "No deadlines, no promises, no future. We aren't in either Germany. We're in Vacqueyras, and that's where we're going to stay."

All he could say was: "Oh, Dorle."

Anything short of total agreement would only bring on even more vociferous pronouncements.

"I have such trust in you," she went on in a low, deep voice. "Fantastic, to be able to trust another person so utterly!"

Dorle! he wanted to cry out in his turn, please don't! But he couldn't say a word.

"I have a feeling I'm floating on a great tide," said Dorle, "that's lifting and lifting me."

"Take me with you," said Wolf.

Very softly she said she didn't want to live beyond this night.

10

AFTER SITTING DOWN in the bus, Wolf found himself once again across from the schoolgirl who always had an open exercise book or textbook on her knees.

So today it was the history book. A photograph of soldiers and mounted officers. She turned the page to reveal a highly agitated Lenin leaning much too far out from the platform. Wolf's immediate thought was: I'll give myself up.

He felt perfectly at home on the morning bus. Today he could see only one Asian woman returning from night duty at the clinic. She was so exhausted that she kept almost falling off her seat. Her face was as dark as it was pale, contorted in her efforts to stay awake; her upper lip would suddenly draw right back from her teeth: combined with the fatigue expressed in the rest of her features, it made her look grotesque. You really ought to avert your eyes, thought Wolf, while aware that he was compelled to watch this pathetic struggle as if spellbound. Simultaneously he was listening to two pensioners arguing with each other. One was entreating the other, who refused to be convinced, to vote for the Free Democratic Party next time, since there was nothing worse than an unfettered Christian Democratic Union. Meanwhile Wolf had been able to detach his gaze from the convulsions in the Asian face and was now watching an anything but attractive woman who had a streaming cold and kept blowing her nose into a long-since saturated paper handkerchief.

Nowhere did Wolf feel as much among his own kind as on the morning bus. Everyone on the bus lacked something. Perhaps they all lacked the same thing. A vision stirred in Wolf's mind: all those who had never ridden a bus during the past three years are picked up by a sorting machine hovering above Bonn. For three years all bus passengers have been sprayed with a trace element. Anyone having no vestige of it is put into a camp. Nothing happens to him; he is merely told that for three years he will not be allowed to hold any public office or fulfill any political function or pursue any profession in which he has power over other people. No reason is given. The decree is intended to be perceived as arbitrary. This is what unites us bus passengers, endows us with our kinship: we are the objects of arbitrary decision. That can be seen by looking at us. But Wolf was quick to tell himself that every three years a completely different, completely unpredictable test must be applied. But conceived by whom? And applied by whom? Since no answer occurred to him, he thought: I'll give myself up.

At this point Wolf turned his attention to a pale young man who was fumbling around at the ticket invalidator, 83 which was apparently out of order. A red light stops the bus, the driver jumps up from his seat, is at the machine, slides in the pale youth's ticket, there is a ping, everyone laughs, the pale young man blushes. I'll give myself up, thought Wolf. Across from him now sat two girls conversing as shyly as if one of them were a man. At last something he could observe with unalloyed pleasure.

As he opened the door to his office, everything he was doing here seemed pointless to him. He was supposed to help with the preparations for the Baden-Württemberg technology exhibit in Moscow. His bookshelf still contained a pile of issues of the periodical *The Soviet Union Today*. He would make suggestions that would compete with suggestions from other departments. The exhibit wasn't pointless. But it probably made no difference whether more square footage were to be occupied with printing technology or with automatic transmissions, whether he would succeed in having the "Servotronic" driving simulator included or whether instead the protective workplace screen would take up more space. There were more satisfying activities than preparing an exhibit. But sometimes even the more satisfying activities suddenly lost their quality of being worthy of recognition. He would refrain from supporting his suggestions by quoting from the Soviet industrial periodical. Although it was also published in German, he kept recalling that scene with the "excellent knowledge of Russian" of a Mr. Stavenhagen. He also recalled his own overreaction to Mr. Borcherdt's "little joke." At the store-minders' party he had made peace with Tiny. He had been obliged to drink four large glasses of a white wine chosen with relentless affability by Tiny, a wine that had tossed him all night long on a heaving ocean with ghastly acid thunderstorms.

Invariably on his first day back at work after a vacation, he was reminded of his first day at school in Leipzig. The feeling that all those around him were united in a conspiracy against him. The telephone jolted him back to Bonn, startling him with its piercing unfamiliar sound. It was Sylvia. She must speak to him, urgently, as soon as possible, today. Five thirty, then. At her place! Siegburger-Strasse.

Wolf got out at the railway station. He had time for a stroll through the inner city. Normally he stopped to look into every store window, as if wanting to buy the very goods displayed there, but today he didn't feel like stopping anywhere. Walking diagonally across the Markt-Platz he suddenly felt a hand on his shoulder. He swung around, prepared for anything. But it was his bookseller, who, on catching sight of Wolf, wanted to tell him that four books in the Workers' Library edition had arrived— two Püschels, two Neutsches—plus the Führmann. "Oh, Mr. Gutzmer!" said Wolf. "Many thanks—I'll drop by tomorrow."

Suddenly he felt very comfortable in Bonn. Could it mean he felt at home here? He would give himself up.

Then when he was standing on Berliner Freiheit waiting for the bus to Beuel, a string of white-and-green police cars and black Mercedes with tinted windows suddenly roared past along Adenauer-Allee, their sirens wailing. The roar came from two helicopters above the motorcade, their lights flashing in a threatening frenzy. The cars were probably racing through the city at that speed in order to thwart assassination attempts. Wolf

85

stood as if paralyzed. So this was now the aura of the state visit. Was it progress for those in power to feel so insecure? An uninhabitable world where the representatives can no longer trust those whom they represent. A ruler murdered today: a sacrifice in the cause of a freedom that an assassin doesn't know what to do with. . . . Miscarried freedom. . . .

Wolf was glad when it came time to get off the bus. Trying to understand people who can kill other people is tormenting. You enter into their motives. Lose your way. Become a murderer.

It turned out that Sylvia had merely wanted to make use of an unexpected absence of Dominick's. Wolf said: "You're going too far, Sylvia. In everything." Here he'd been worrying about what could possibly have happened. So she'd only wanted to sleep with him. "Only?" she said. If she didn't blackmail Wolf he wouldn't come, and if he didn't come she would die, so rather than die she blackmailed him. She'd had no idea, when it all started between them, that things would ever get this far. She had never before bared herself so emotionally to anyone. As she spoke he remembered Dorle saying that Sylvia was "cheap." When Dorle had been taking up a collection in Section 211 to send flowers to Mrs. Meissner on the birth of her fourth child, Sylvia had exclaimed: "You can give Dr. Meissner my regards—the only money he'll see from me is for condoms." Again Dorle found that "cheap." Wolf had been impressed by this typical Sylvia-outburst.

By this time Sylvia was on the subject of Dominick. Whenever she and Wolf met, she had to talk a lot about Dominick. And Wolf really had to listen. Sometimes she would stop quite abruptly and ask: "What did I just say?" If he hadn't been listening she would dissolve into tears and sobs. So now he always listened attentively. Every word, every gesture, she said, affected Dominick in exactly the opposite way to what one intended. Perhaps it was time for Dominick to change psychiatrists again, said Wolf. "Every psychiatrist is a psychiatrist," said Sylvia. His fits of panic were no longer quite so bad. He had been able to masturbate again. The present psychiatrist had accomplished that. However, she doubted whether he meant to accomplish much more than that.

Then she wanted to hear from Wolf yet again that it was only at first that he had come to her because of the protocols. By this time he was coming for her sake—or wasn't he? He admitted it. But even so he could only sleep with her under duress, he said. Only when she blackmailed him. She had to say: Sleep with me or I'll denounce you. "I believe you'll soon be needing a psychiatrist too," she said. "Say it," he said. She said it. "OK," he said, "come on, you morass, you." If he was going to call her names, she said, he should call her Clitoris. That was the most beautiful name for a woman that she knew. If her mother had been honest, she should have had her baptized Clitoris. "If you'll talk a little less I'll call you Clitoris," he said. That made her smile as if in bliss, her eyes closed in ecstasy. Even if she's only pretending all this, he thought, she does it very well. Perhaps intercourse between the sexes is the only thing in the world where no difference exists between the real thing and pretense.

But my God, it was time for him to go. Sylvia's awareness of reality was underdeveloped and could easily be almost entirely extinguished by other sensual perceptions.

While he was crossing the Rhine again by bus, he felt glad that Dorle and Sylvia were at least separated by the Rhine. He belonged over there, on the left bank, to Dorle. He felt that more clearly than ever. With Sylvia he really couldn't spend any time at all. Until they were actually in bed they talked and laughed merrily enough, but afterward he really had to get away as quickly as possible. Come to think of it, there was nothing about Sylvia that he could still find bearable. That seemed unfair to him, but that's how it was. In any case the Rhine couldn't be wide enough for him. It gave him a good feeling to see the Rhine churning along there so powerfully, as if it were being paid by the ton for mass transportation of water. Looking back, Wolf could see a barge, one man standing upright at the wheel, another hosing down the deck. Wolf wished he could be one of them. But, he told himself, it's enough to breathe freely, to say the date, and to look at the door without fear: then you'll be comfortable with your part of the world, that's where you belong. Give yourself up!

11

DORLE WAS BANGING about in the kitchen. He could hear this the second he opened their front door. She didn't even know he was back, yet she was already banging about. He was sure she didn't know how much reason she had for banging. She was throwing saucepan lids around, slamming cupboard doors shut. He was to blame for this outburst, which apparently hadn't yet reached its climax. Wolf quickly went over to her and put his arms around her; she shook him off. He admired her sensitivity. Some people are sensitive to the weather, others are sensitive even to fate.

"I'm sorry," she said. No, no, he wanted to say, you don't have to apologize, you're so very right. She couldn't find a thing since they'd got back, she said. "Oh, Dorle," he said. He shouldn't be just looking on. He should be telling her that she had every reason in the world for banging about in such misery. She shouldn't reproach herself, please. It wasn't because of a few kitchen trifles that she was beside herself. But he couldn't say anything.

She had been waiting for him. "I know," he said. "Come," she said, picked up her handbag, and led him out of the kitchen and out of the apartment. Never mind where to, he thought, he'd follow. Even if she led him to Sylvia. There had to be an end, finally, to everything. She went to the car, drove up the curving road into the forest as far as the Cassel's Ruhe restaurant, parked the car, got out, walked off into the forest; he followed. She walked as she had driven: too fast. He had to catch up with her. But she maintained her speed until they were above Bad Godesberg. Only at that point did she decide she didn't want to go down into Bad Godesberg; she turned around and walked back just as abruptly and relentlessly.

She had fled from the apartment in such a hurry, she said, because she was now quite sure they were under surveillance. While they had been in France, bugs had been installed in the apartment. If not earlier. And Dr. Meissner is the source of her information. He hadn't come right out with it; of course he can't do that. That would be suicide. But he had asked her to come to his office, after all the others had left, and had poured himself a glass of red wine; when he had wanted to pour her one, she had shaken her head. I must talk to you, he had said—that's to say, I should. But I can't! he had burst out. In despair. I can't, Doris, I . . . can't . . . do it. How long could he keep this up, this I must and I can't? Could she tell him that? What I'd really like to do is blackmail you, he'd then gone on. Can you be blackmailed? Those were his next words. Then he had suddenly changed the subject: How had their vacation been? At her brother's? This time they hadn't gone to her brother's, she had said. He: Not this time? Oh. Why not this time? She, without hesitation: There's been a fire in my brother's tower in the Têt valley. Luckily there really had been a fire there at Whitsun.

"I don't know what I'd have done if I hadn't had that fire." "You would have invented one," said Wolf quite calmly. "Invented one!" she cried, her voice almost shrill. "You're crazy," she said, "you've no idea. You still believe it's possible to invent something. Anything invented is without substance. When are you going to realize that? The truth simply will prevail," she said. "Like fire. Or water."

"So what did you answer, when he asked whether you could be blackmailed?" asked Wolf. "Go ahead and try!" I told him. "Very good," said Wolf. "And then?" Well, she had told him about Istres, said it was lovely though much too noisy at night, the water awful, but the Napoleon beach, the mistral, the sea, the sand! She had felt she must simply go on talking just so Dr. Meissner couldn't get in another word. "And?" asked Wolf. Meissner had listened, but he'd looked at her in such a way that she no longer knew whether he was really listening. At some point he had said: Oh, Dorle, I'm not a computer, you know! "And then?" "Then we parted company. It was obvious he couldn't go on. Oh, Dorle, I'm not a computer, you know. More than that he couldn't say. He so badly wants to tell me that we're under surveillance, but he mustn't, and that's his agony. Because he likes me."

Wolf was relieved. On the one hand. Dr. Meissner knew nothing: that could be assumed from all that Dorle had told him. On the other hand, Dorle was obviously in a terrible state, which she attributed to completely false reasons. That might be even more dangerous than if she had been thinking in the direction from which her panic originated. The first thing Wolf had to do was defuse her alarm. Even if everything were the way she believed—she had never done anything, he said. She was married to him. That wasn't a crime. In his jargon she was a contact person, she said, through her he . . . "Nonsense," he said. "I don't need you to get at your colleagues." "Don't brag," she said. Wolf explained in detail that he was perhaps the very first scout whose cover by this time corresponded almost completely to the truth. He had slapped his professor, had been kicked out of university, and had gone off to the West. No one could possibly know that, prior to his departure, the State Security Service had approached him. But if it would make her feel better, he would report her suspicions to Normannen-Strasse, they had people over here in counterespionage who can find out easily enough whether there is anything on him. No, she doesn't want that, certainly not that. "Aha!" he said. "Like every paranoid you want to protect your delusion from the truth that might threaten it. Or what other reason do you have for not wanting to make sure?" She simply doesn't want that. Aha, so she wants him to be blown, as the jargon has it. "Yes, you idiot!" "So why don't you want any inquiries made?" She simply feels that it would be wrong to ask questions over there so that they in turn would ask questions over here. That's against her instincts. All right, so he won't. Up to now he has always gone by her instincts. But then what's he supposed to do? When she sounds the alarm like that! How does she expect him to react? "Not at all," she says. "For the time being." She'll straighten it out. Even if she has to sleep with Dr. Meissner. "Oh," he says. "Would you have any objection?" she asks. "If I remember correctly, we've discussed every angle of this some ninety-nine times," he replies. "But without ever coming to a clear-cut result," she says. He has no comment.

When they got back into the car at the Cassel's Ruhe she said: "Not a word about this in the apartment." He nodded, although he felt that this was tantamount to agreeing with her, and that was exactly what he didn't want. But he couldn't change her mood. It was the only thing this racing through the forest had demonstrated.

That evening he read the Schiller play alone. And Dorle didn't move across to him when he picked up the paperback. He had the feeling that he was asking Schiller for sanctuary.

> Woe, woe is me! if e'er my hand should wield
> The avenging sword of God, and my vain heart
> Cherish affection to a mortal man!
> 'Twere better for me I had ne'er been born!
> Henceforth no more of this, unless ye would
> Provoke the Spirit's wrath who in me dwells!
> The eye of man, regarding me with love,
> To me is horror and profanity.

12

On Friday evening of that week Wolf got off the bus at the railway station, picked up the five books, then walked along Kaiser-Strasse looking for the legal offices of Bestenhorn & Buhl. The waiting room: empty. It was after office hours. Then a voice called out: "Please come in!" He was startled. He could still turn back. But there he was, already seated, thanking Mr. Bestenhorn for seeing him at this hour. His name was Buhl, said the attorney, he was Mr. Bestenhorn's partner. On Fridays at this time Mr. Bestenhorn was already airborne. This fellow Buhl looked like the people on the bus. He offered Wolf a cigarette. Judging by the ashtray, the smell in the room, and his appearance, Mr. Buhl smoked incessantly. Wolf declined. In that man's company, no cigarette would give him any pleasure: he would be enough to make anyone quit.

Wolf said he had come about a friend, his best friend, in fact, who yesterday had turned up, or rather burst in—anyway Wolf had had quite a shock when his friend

suddenly stood there in the doorway and announced—
well, Wolf had thought the roof would fall in on him
when his friend blurted out—and now he, Wolf, was
about to repeat it just as starkly, as unvarnished, as his
friend had announced it to Wolf, his oldest friend, after
making sure that Wolf's wife wasn't in the apartment,
he'd come straight out with it: he was an agent. And
why is he suddenly coming out with it now? He wants
to give himself up. But how? What does he have to be
prepared for? Which form of capitulation is likely to en-
tail the lightest sentence? And—this seemed to be his
chief concern—must his wife be prepared for punishment too? Also, his friend says, only the local authorities
are to know that he is giving himself up. His former
employers in the East are to receive the impression that
he's been blown, has been caught. He doesn't want ever
to be exchanged, he says. That, too, is not to be mentioned in court. Also, he does not need to involve anyone
else; he has been working completely on his own. He
will not reveal the names of those who helped him.
Without him they will do nothing illegal.

Mr. Buhl had been making notes. Now he looked up
because Wolf had stopped speaking.

"Are you your friend?" he asked.

Wolf said: "Yes."

13

On his way home Wolf got out at Poppelsdorf Center, one stop earlier than usual. At the Akropolis there were so few customers that the owner was again killing time at the pinball machine. Wolf phoned Dorle and asked her to come down, to the Akropolis. Dorle refused. Wolf called the owner to the phone, knowing that the man had always impressed Dorle by employing his entire family in the establishment, as was evident to all the customers. Whoever entered the Akropolis took part willy-nilly in the family life. But no matter how hard the owner tried, Dorle wouldn't come. Wolf drank up his beer, paid, and walked home up the hill. He would rather have told Dorle in the bar. He was scared. On the way home he recited Schiller's lines of Joan's soliloquy after having looked at Lionel, the young English knight:

> With that glance,
> Thy crime, thy woe commenced. Unhappy
> one!

A sightless instrument thy God demands,
Blindly thou must accomplish his behest!
When thou didst see, God's shield abandoned
    thee,
And the dire snares of hell around thee
    pressed!

He had read these lines over and over again. They spelled out his case against the sky like giant projectors. The ruthless resolve of these lines gave him a good feeling. No discussion possible. Either—or. That was it.

He positively basked in this resolve.

Dorle had become suspicious, but he couldn't start telling her right away. Surely it's all right to drop in at the Greek's on a Friday evening, isn't it? "But not like that," said Dorle. She's sitting around at home, he was due home long ago, then he calls up from the Greek's—no thanks. He told her he had simply wanted to carry on with what they had been discussing that evening and that night in Vacqueyras. The trust that Dorle had so ardently proclaimed there was weighing on him. "Oh, really?" said Dorle. "Come off it," he said. She couldn't remember it that clearly, she said, maybe she'd simply had too much to drink. "But what did we drink to?" he asked. To total trust, and that was a bigger burden than he could bear. Oh, she'd be glad to release him from that: not for a second had she really trusted him, not for a second. She had only staged that outburst of trust in order to point up what he was doing. "But you did trust me," he said, "you did believe that I only see Sylvia because of the protocols." No, she didn't. Wolf: But it had been like that at first, only now, recently . . . She interrupted him. "Don't bother!" she cried, she could do without such explanations. "I have a husband who goes to another woman. There is no reason that can justify that. Not one!" Then why did she go along with it? Why didn't she simply leave him? Because she still didn't grasp it, she said. She had no other explanation. It had taken a few years for her really to be able to believe him when he told her that he had married her not merely because she was a secretary at the Ministry. But he had accomplished that. She believed now that he liked her. That he was seeing or had to see another woman or several other women was his business. He had explained to her a thousand times why he had to do that. She had never once understood how he could do such a thing. For her it was sheer hell. How long she could stand it she didn't know.

She could breathe freely again, he said, it was over, he had given himself up.

She jumped up, stood, went to him, practically collapsed over him, then burst into tears. Never before had she cried like that. It was like a natural disaster. An upheaval, a melting through and through, an opening of the floodgates. A sobbing that seemed to mount from one intensification to the next. Everything had to find its way out now in a torrent of tears. Much of it was choked, strangled, had to be pressed out, forced out, screamed out. Really—never had she screamed like that. Never had he heard anyone scream like that. Never had he wanted to be as close to anyone. Never had he been so helpless. He could feel himself trembling. Through and through. All solidity gone. He had no substance. If she didn't immediately become aware of him. She must show him immediately that he meant something to her. Otherwise he was nothing. If she didn't extend her weeping to him right now, include him in it, or at least allow him to enter it, then ... There is not only a concussion of the brain, there is also a concussion of the soul. He couldn't exist like that. He had to reach out for her. He had to make her aware of him. He had to beg her to take him in. He recalled two more lines of Schiller:

> Couldst thou
> Behold mine inmost heart, thou, shuddering,
> Wouldst fly the traitoress, the enemy!

He longed to declaim them now in his driest, brightest voice, but it was no longer possible to talk. Only to feel one's way, search for a foothold, for a support. But it would take a while before either of them would convey to the other by some minimal gesture an awareness of the presence of the other. When Dorle was gradually left with only the convulsive breathing that followed upon her weeping fit, he said he hoped he'd be able to stick it out. "Somewhere I'll have to face a court," he said, "either over there or here. I prefer here."

With immense pauses, and gasping for air between the words, Dorle said: "The country where one would rather face a court is the one to choose. Perhaps."

Since the radio was switched to receiving and it was

Friday, nine thirty, he heard his signal, and the soprano sang:

> And now abideth faith, hope, charity,
> These three; but the greatest of these
> Is charity.

Wolf hurried across, switched off. Thank you, he said, emphasizing the second word.

14

JUST AS WOLF was approaching his front door he heard Mr. Ujfalussy call out: "Mr. Zieger, have you moment?" He'll never lose that, long after he knows better, Wolf thought. Out of affection for his native land. Wolf envied Mr. Ujfalussy his indestructible, never-to-be-doubted Hungarianness.

He asked Wolf to sit down. Dispensing with an article and stressing the first syllable, he had surprise for Wolf. Wolf said he was in a terrible hurry. "Oh, please!" cried the Hungarian, now that he had *re*sult, with *math*ematical-logical method: a man who plays *p*iano so well, but does not dare play, must be *af*raid of *sur*roundings, and who is *af*raid of *sur*roundings if he is otherwise normal? The spy! Mr. Zieger, according to *math*ematical-logical method, you must be spy!" Ujfalussy laughed immoderately, apologized, and said he had brought a few bottles of wine from his native country for Mr. Zieger and charming Mrs. Zieger. The Ziegers were such delightful neighbors. Always playing the piano with only one hand, such admirable consideration. He hoped the Ziegers would enjoy the Hungarian wine. Wolf said they would all drink it together. "That would be a great pleasure for me, Mr. Zieger," said Mr. Ujfalussy.

15

THE FIRST TIME Wolf sat across from Dorle in the visitors' room he thought he wouldn't be able to get out a word. Four visitors sat facing four prisoners. At the head of the table, a guard. But after only a few seconds the visitors and prisoners to left and right of him were so occupied with one another, so concentrated upon one another, that he actually felt he was alone here with Dorle. If there was anything that didn't interest those to left and right, it was himself and Dorle. "Say something," he said, after the two of them had sat facing each other for a while without saying a word.

Dorle described how she had been picked up for her first interrogation. She had thought she was being arrested so had asked Dr. Meissner in the presence of the police officer to take charge of the tape she had been keeping in her desk. But her boss didn't want the tape. She had told him the tape was strictly private, concerned only him, no one apart from himself should listen to it. She had been wanting to give it to him for a long time.

That almost looked like a conspiracy, Dr. Meissner had said, and had suggested, in order to eliminate any suspicion, that they listen to it together with Chief Inspector Ruhfuss. Impossible, she had exclaimed! The tape was extremely private. Well then, what do we do? Dr. Meissner had asked. The police officer had suggested that Dr. Meissner could listen to the tape alone, and that if he found that it was not strictly private he could phone him at his office in Meckenheim. Dr. Meissner considered that an ingenious solution. At this point Wolf should have told Dorle that during his second interrogation the chief inspector had played him a tape that had been made in the Senats-Hotel in Cologne. He couldn't bring himself to do it. That night, after his return from the attorney's office, they had promised each other from now on to face everything together. Luckily Dorle went right on with her story. Dr. Meissner's amateurish attempts to feign surprise when the police officer showed up was for her a proof that Dr. Meissner hadn't been surprised at all. Wolf said that this had meanwhile been confirmed to him, too: they had been under surveillance for several years. Like rats in a laboratory, he said. "What's the matter?" he asked, when Dorle didn't continue.

She didn't know how to say it, but, well, she was pregnant. "Oh?" said Wolf. "Yes," she said. "What wonderful news," said Wolf. "Yes," said Dorle. "Aren't you glad?" asked Wolf. "Of course I'm glad," said Dorle. "Then show that you're glad!" Wolf insisted. "That's not so easy," she replied, "under the circumstances." "I should really have noticed it myself," said Wolf. "You look like something just beginning to grow."

104

16

SITTING AND STARING uses up a lot of time, thought Wolf. He had too little time. He had refused Sylvia's visit. Now he reproached himself for that. It had been right to refuse Sylvia's visit; it would have been even more right to accept it. But if Dorle were to find out. And Sylvia would have seen to it that Dorle did find out. Never again must he return to that illegitimate state. That no man's land. Every second of life destroyed to the very marrow. Nothing is what it seems. Everything totally damaged. The illegitimate state reaches everywhere. Every mouthful, every drink, is swallowed by a person whose senses are half-benumbed. Counterarguments can be used to dispute the hollowing-out effect of the illegal state. The illegitimate state is oneself.

Now he felt that he was perceiving himself with a kind of disapproval of which he couldn't get enough. No one but he was allowed to disapprove of himself to such an extent, but *he* was allowed to do so as much as he liked.

It was no use pretending that he had, as it were, put

Sylvia behind him. But he would never see her again. Maybe at the actual trial. Then never again. He would be sorry, but that was all. Sylvia obviously had a gift for discerning a man's wishes and then fulfilling them. He would have to try to get Dorle to that point. But he would be sorry for Dorle if she did everything he would like her to do. When you love a person, you want to protect that person from yourself. He'll get along without Sylvia's services. The pleasant thing about Sylvia is that in her case they aren't services. That's the way she is. She is a discoverer, an exploiter, a satisfier. Actually she is very demanding. He must write to her. Or was that already a trap? Was he trying to make an impression? He had to learn to accept the fact that she felt ill-used. Ill-used by him. His capacity for self-respect was apparently tied to a kind of loyalty to Dorle. He had lived long enough in the grueling state of self-rejection. Being in remand custody was a pleasant experience compared with his mood in the no man's land of illegitimacy.

He wrote to his father, who had known nothing of Wolf's covert activities. Wolf wrote that he had been arrested. He knew that Comrade Bergmann would read his letter. Although the fact of his turning himself in would be taken into account at the trial, it would not be mentioned at the public hearing. That had been agreed. He wrote his father saying he would be happy if the reasons that had put him into prison bore comparison with those that had put his father into a concentration camp. He would like to talk to his father about it, later, when he had served his sentence. Comrade Bergmann could interpret that as a desire to be speedily exchanged. To make it quite unmistakable for State Security eyes, he ended with: "We'll meet again, even if it has to be at the border crossing at Herleshausen."

Since being in prison, Wolf had been thinking more about his father than ever before. Wolf's mother had died from the consequences of a ruptured spleen, caused by a fall from a bicycle. He could scarcely remember her. His father's last job had been shift foreman in a dairy commune. But the development of music for wind instruments had apparently interested him more than improvements in milking techniques. He had been given early retirement and was finally able to devote himself entirely to his music. When Wolf had said goodbye to him fifteen years ago, his father had nodded; he would have preferred to see Wolf becoming an organist. Father's father had been an organist in Memel. A Zieger choir was said to have been in existence in Memel right up to the war. His great-great-grandfather apparently reached Memel around the middle of the last century, after an arduous three-months' journey—meanwhile romanticized by fading memory and eager retelling—via Stettin, Stargard, Praust, Danzig, Marienburg, Elbing, Königsberg, and Pillau. Before Wolf's father could follow the musical tradition of the family he had had to help drive the Soviet revolutionaries out of Riga; after that to flee. To the German Reich. He had always spoken of himself as someone who had been cheated out of his career. He wanted his son to return to music.

His father shouldn't have felt pity for Riga and Reval in 1919, nor for the prisoners in the Buchenwald concentration camp in 1939. After 1945 he had apparently made an effort to conform, principally by remaining silent. He had once told Wolf how the Russians had given orders that potatoes be planted at a depth of half a meter. The people had known this to be wrong but had done as they were ordered. The harvest had been almost a total failure. After telling this story he had made Wolf promise not to repeat it in school.

His father consisted of a jumble of random details. A powder-blackened face when he fought his way across a bridge in Memel or Riga or Reval and then on the other side turned around a cannon to fire after the fleeing enemy. When Wolf listened to West Germans discussing why the first verse of "Deutschland über alles," with its line "From the Maas up to the Memel," was no longer appropriate, he had to think of his great-great-grandfather, who had played the organ in Memel and founded a choir. . . . Not that he wanted Memel back. He wanted to be allowed to regret the loss. To be allowed to say: how wonderful if we still had it! That's what he wanted. East and West Germans seemed to him like distortions of something that no longer existed. All that was left was excrescences, he thought, over there as well as here. The lost. They have lost themselves. Each person notices it in the other but not in himself. Whatever is lost in Leipzig is noticed by everyone from Stuttgart who comes to Leipzig. Whatever Stuttgart loses is noticed by the person from Leipzig coming to Stuttgart. Wolf remembered the evening when, coming from Stuttgart, he had got off the train in Bonn and all the other travelers had suddenly seemed to him like half-people. Once he had served his sentence he would give up such notions. He had resisted adaptation long enough. But he had adapted. And in Fellbach and Strümpfelbach he would adapt completely. He would tell his children about their grandfather, an East Prussian who ended up living in Thuringia, the last ethicist in the family.

When Mr. Buhl, the partner, pleaded with him to announce publicly at the trial that he did not wish to be exchanged, Wolf refused. Mr. Buhl told him that even the length of the sentence depended upon this. The court would assume that after conviction the defendant would be taken home within a few short years, via Herleshausen. And for the court there was no more impressive proof of the defendant's conversion than declining to be exchanged. Even the prosecutor could be affected by a timely statement in this respect. Wolf said he couldn't do the powers-that-be this favor. The powers-that-be didn't care one way or another, said the attorney; Wolf would merely be harming his own cause. Wolf said he wasn't going to turn his decision to remain here into a political trade-off. Buhl was apparently scared of his Mr. Bestenhorn. He indicated to Wolf that Mr. Bestenhorn would accuse him, Buhl, of being incapable of anything, even of obtaining something as straightforward as this statement—that the defendant wished to remain in the West. Wolf said there were a few people in the GDR who would feel hurt if he publicly stated that he wished to stay here. He was thinking of the general. But also of Bergmann. Could he quote him on that, asked Buhl? "No," said Wolf.

17

Shortly before the trial opened, Wolf was transferred to Düsseldorf. His case was to be heard before the Fourth Branch of the Düsseldorf Superior Court, the branch responsible for state security. Wolf felt as well prepared as an athlete who, throughout a long training period, has done all that he should, made no mistakes, and wishes only that now he may finally be allowed to show what excellent shape he is in.

Wolf sat quietly in a room in the basement of the Superior Court, examining his fingernails. They would pass muster. The policeman who had brought him here was reading the *BILD-Zeitung*. The man looked ill, thought Wolf, his face was sallow. Next door a typewriter was stuttering under the two fingers of another official, but it fairly raced along when underlining. These are now the events in his life. For how long? For how many years? There was a knock at the door. Mr. Buhl. In his gown Buhl looked like a villain in disguise. Today he was smoking as frantically as if he had to stock up on smoking in view of the imminent smokeless hours in court. He wore a white tie. Just wanted to say Hello, he said, that was all. And to warn Wolf not to be overawed. Justitia was a goddess of the theater. The idea was to soften up the accused, to make him regard his own interest as minor when compared to some greater, loftier, mist-shrouded interest of the state. . . .

Mr. Bestenhorn came into the room. Buhl immediately stopped speaking, immediately stubbed out his cigarette. Wolf had never seen Buhl smoking in Mr. Bestenhorn's presence. Bestenhorn was about the same age as Wolf. He had planned a strategy whereby Wolf was to be saved, or at least preserved from the worst— which would be a ten-year prison sentence.

During these preparatory meetings, Mr. Bestenhorn had always treated Wolf as if Wolf were a classmate of his to whom Bestenhorn, the brightest boy in the class, gave special coaching in all subjects out of the goodness of his heart. But if Wolf were to fail in spite of this, the brightest boy would hold it very much against him since his own reputation was at stake. Whatever he put his hand to *must* succeed, he insisted on that. In his gown Bestenhorn looked like a movie star about to play a courtroom scene—although his chin really did project beyond any role. Mr. Bestenhorn kept Wolf's hand in his own for as long as he was in the room. Today for the first time Wolf sensed a kind of warmth, perhaps even solidarity. Wolf felt protected.

He could entrust his fate to this strong contemporary of his. Buhl, twenty or thirty years his senior, stood there nodding and looking even more miserable when he wasn't smoking. Mr. Bestenhorn also had some good news: because Dorle is pregnant, the court has granted Bestenhorn's application to have the proceedings against Sylvia Wellershoff treated separately. "We must show some gratitude to the presiding judge for that," said Mr. Bestenhorn, "but not too much." From outside came the voice of the usher of the court calling upon everyone concerned with the case of Doris and Wolfgang Zieger to be seated. The attorneys hurried out; they had to enter the courtroom by a different door from the one used by Wolf and the police escort.

When Wolf was ushered into the courtroom and shown his seat, the room was already full of people. He avoided looking at anyone. He was glad that, while seated in the dock, he had his back turned to the room. He and Dorle had agreed that they would give each other a friendly nod. But please, no emotional display. No drama, of any kind whatever. The prosecuting attorney had already taken her place, over to the right as seen from the spectators' seats. To the left, the table for the defense. The panel of judges filed in. Five dignified men in their handsome robes. The presiding judge wasn't a day older than Wolf or Mr. Bestenhorn. They all, including the prosecuting attorney, seemed to have been born in the same year. That affected Wolf like warmth on a chilly day. And as for the usher, who sat down between the judges and the prosecuting attorney, he couldn't have been thirty! A cheerful Rhenish fellow with a mop of curly hair. And the presiding judge appeared to be quite shy, or embarrassed, when he called upon all those who had risen at the judges' entrance please to be seated again. He had a rather soft, breathy voice that immediately rose in pitch whenever he tried to speak louder.

And the way he was asking for not too much formality in this and all future appearances of the court seemed to imply that, if it were up to him, such rituals would long since have been abolished. The issue here was, after all, more important than standing up and sitting down, wasn't it?

Wolf felt deeply drawn to this presiding judge, a man of his own age. His accent seemed to indicate that he came from East Prussia, or that his parents came from there and he had inherited some of that delightful propensity to spread himself in the vowels and breathily soften the consonants. The proceedings were opened by the presiding judge presenting Wolf's life history. To Wolf's ears it sounded as if the judge's voice had vibrated sympathetically in reading out the sentences that dealt with Wolf's father, who had been forced by political circumstances to move from East Prussia to Thuringia in the early twenties. Buchenwald, too, was mentioned. Wolf's father was extolled. Wolf found the tone of this praise just right.

Wolf's own history was presented by the judge as if the latter deplored that everything had had to happen the way it did. Wolf kept looking across at the judge, but without managing to establish eye contact with him. Wolf even gained the impression that the judge was deliberately avoiding any eye contact. But Wolf felt that this man understood him.

Wolf would have liked to express agreement with everything he was saying. The judge had obviously spent months delving with unflagging energy into everything that Wolf had told the Federal Criminal Investigation officials in Meckenheim in countless interrogations.

Time and again the judge proved that he knew more about Wolf's life and activities than anyone else in the courtroom. Maybe even more than Wolf himself. This man was simply insatiable when it came to accuracy and correctness. Any trial he presided over appeared to be conducted before the eyes of a supreme world court that was already in possession of a matchless complete fund of knowledge. In the eyes of this world court, any trial presided over by this judge must be seen to be without flaw, without error. For that reason and for that reason alone, he had to persist in his questioning of Wolf, in order that the trial and its protocol would be free of any flaw or any error.

Did Wolf happen to know, the judge asked, with which unit his father had fought against the Soviets for the protection of East Prussia? With the Baltic regiment, said Wolf. Was Wolf sure that his father had participated in the liberation of Riga? Yes. In that case his father had been what was known as a Baltic fighter, that is, a member of the volunteer corps. The Baltic regiment had protected Reval, not liberated Riga. And if Wolf's father had later found refuge on the Schwerstedt estate in Thuringia, that also implied a volunteer corps background. The judge liked to end such interpolations by remarking in a voice barely more than a sigh: It doesn't make life any easier when one refuses to go along with the general confusion between Latvia and Estonia.

The judge was able to quote from the six volumes of the interrogation protocol, the two volumes of the recorded wiretapping protocol, and the two volumes of surveillance reports, without ever having to consult them. He had familiarized himself with Dr. Bruno's affidavits and those of the Dutch supplier of Dr. Bruno's engineering company, and he could request the usher to produce such exhibits as notes, railway tickets, handwriting specimens: he was indeed the master of the proceedings.

And Wolf felt with gratitude that the judge was protecting him against the imputatory zeal of the prosecuting attorney. This elegant, beautiful, red-haired lady always came into the courtroom through the public entrance, and she always carried her gown, which was trimmed with more velvet than the presiding judge's, over her arm as she came in. A bell skirt swinging with her temperamental stride, boots the color of her hair, the proud, aquiline face of a handsome bird of prey— that was her daily appearance, which she then crowned by slipping into her gown only after arriving at her seat.

Wolf gradually came to believe that she hated him or loathed him. Just as the judge seemed to like Wolf in terms of his life history, so this woman obviously disliked him to the same degree in terms of everything he was and had done. Sometimes she put questions to him that could only be meant to destroy his credibility. Often he noticed this too late: "Did you after your arrest have any further contact with Mrs. Wellershoff?" she asked. Wolf denied that he had. And she immediately proved the contrary. In the proceedings, to spare Mrs. Wellershoff from being arrested, it had been stipulated—and the accused had been so informed—that there was to be no contact whatever, yet the accused had smuggled out a letter to Mrs. Wellershoff. Wolf had to admit this and knew that it would be futile to describe the letter as a purely personal communication. The prosecuting attorney turned everything she said into a triumph. She didn't even spare the presiding judge if she saw a chance to demonstrate her superiority. When Mr. Bestenhorn, as agreed with Wolf, asked whether his obtaining the MRS 903 might represent a serious setback to the ECM technology, the judge mildly interrupted to ask what ECM meant. And quick as a flash came from her: "Electronic Counter-Measures, your honor." Whereupon the judge, as if ashamed to have to put into words what he now unfortunately had to say, barely more than murmured: "I know that, my learned friend, I merely asked so that the answer would mean one less abbreviation in the record." And now really only in a whisper: "If there were something I could hate, it would be abbreviations." From that moment on, Wolf used no more abbreviations in replying to the judge. As for the prosecuting attorney, he answered her only with abbreviations. And when at one point she became irritable because she didn't understand what ZSGL of the FDJ meant and asked him whether he meant to annoy her with these abbreviations, he replied that he happened to come from a country that was unable to fill its quotas without ABREMA. Turning to the presiding judge he translated blandly, as if in parenthesis: abbreviation mania.

After the first week, Mr. Bestenhorn demanded that Wolf change his mental attitude toward the presiding judge. Wolf was on the point, he said, of falling into the trap laid by this understatement-virtuoso. For a whole week now Wolf had been admitting and confirming everything just the way the judge wanted it admitted and confirmed. After this first week the score was 1:0 in the court's favor. The judge was much more cunning than

Wolf could possibly imagine. The judge gave the impression of being solely concerned with the correctness of barely relevant, minute details. When did you arrive in Venlo? Was it only in St. Willibrod that you thought of skipping the meeting with Kercher? Or did you want to circumvent Dr. Bruno and get to the Dutch supplier yourself? Thus the judge, questioning, murmuring, questioning with infinite gentleness. And Wolf docilely giving exactly the answers the judge wished to hear. Out of these myriad details the judge was weaving a terribly ominous web in which eventually Wolf Zieger would be hopelessly caught as a convinced activist representing a threat to the state.

Wolf almost had the impression that Bestenhorn was jealous of the presiding judge. This flattered him. Wolf was absolutely sure that Mr. Bestenhorn was mistaken. But he didn't contradict him. Mr. Bestenhorn was simply prejudiced by the routine of his role. And by his strategy, which he now once again dinned into Wolf. What Mr. Bestenhorn had prepared for Wolf was a role. Son of a man repeatedly frustrated and damaged by politics, yet idealistic from the very beginning; next a student's prank, then the serious consequences of this prank are exploited by the State Security Service for purposes of blackmail. Wolf pretends to agree, only after arrival in the West does he perceive the fatal trend of the German partition, now he really does want to help, but he fails; apart from fake material he has sent almost nothing across, himself a pawn of the rival German State Security Services, himself a grotesque product of the increasingly grotesque German-German polarization—until he decides to bail out from this disastrous German-German rivalry, from now on to think only of his wife, of himself, of their future child, their future children.

Wolf knew the role, knew it by heart, and was looking forward to performing it in public and some of it with the public excluded: it was not merely a role, after all, although due to Bestenhorn's direction many of the contradictions had been removed. However, Wolf also wanted to react to what was happening at the trial, he wanted to adjust to this presiding judge, this prosecuting attorney. He believed that Bestenhorn's strategy as such was becoming too obvious, too tendentious, hence lacking in credibility. He wanted to be truly understood by the judge, even in all the contradictions and irrationalities in which he had entangled himself over the years. He believed that the sentence would be less severe if the presiding judge and associate judges understood him than if with Bestenhorn's help he presented a case so crafted that it more or less ensured the mildest possible sentence under Paragraphs 92 to 101.

Wolf wanted to be understood and then leave the judgment to the understanding of the court. He wanted to be able to trust. Bestenhorn trusted nothing but what he could do himself. And he could obviously do a great deal. He was invariably successful. Wolf had had ample evidence of this from watching Buhl, the disheveled partner. Whenever Bestenhorn spoke, Buhl involuntarily started to nod in agreement and confirmation. Bestenhorn had produced Buhl's nodding through his actions and behavior, and now he obviously expected it from the rest of the world. Wolf didn't want to interfere with Bestenhorn's notion of success; he merely wanted to shore it up, on the human side. That was, as it were, his task.

And his interest. He mustn't restrict himself to an attorney's vision.

Before the five members of the panel filed in on Monday for the second week of the trial, before Dorle had taken her seat, Bestenhorn came hurrying over to Wolf to tell him that Dr. Bruno had died. Yesterday evening. He had only heard it himself on coming in. "That can only be to our advantage," he said with an affable nod, then nimbly regained his place as the panel filed in, and the frail presiding judge, who today looked almost noble, indicated by means of minimal gestures to all those who had risen that it was not he who expected let alone demanded them to rise. The presiding judge even had a special gesture for Mr. Bestenhorn, who, in spite of all his nimbleness, hadn't quite reached his seat by the time the panel had almost reached theirs. Please take your time, he had indicated to the attorney. Nowhere in the world is there to be a more relaxed atmosphere than in a courtroom over which I preside.

"We will continue in the case against Mr. and Mrs. Zieger," he said pensively and through his nose. Nevertheless Wolf smarted at the word "against." Each time this judge opened a session, this "against" occurred, and Wolf felt hurt. The curly haired Rhenish usher, as soon as he had lugged in the bin of files, always called out: "Please be seated for the Zieger case!" Wolf liked that much better. It sounded like a request to go to the dining car. On this point the distinguished judge was a little insensitive. He began:

"We will now proceed to the reading of the statements of Dr. Rick Bruno, who is prevented by illness from appearing in court." Instantly Bestenhorn was on his feet to report: "Your honor, Dr. Bruno died yesterday evening." The judge immediately acquired a genuinely grieved expression; his little hands protruding from the sleeves of his robe fluttered with dismay. "Oh dear," he said, "how sad!" And in a tone that was a virtual apology for what had to be said, he went on: "According to Paragraph 251, Section 1, Numbers 1 and 4, with the consent of those involved in the case, the statements of the witness Dr. Rick Bruno, who is prevented by death from attending, may be admitted as evidence by reading out the verbatim record of the judicial interrogation of that witness." There being no challenge to this, one of the associate judges read out what had come to light at Dr. Bruno's interrogation. An expert opinion supplied by the medical officer in attendance at the interrogations was also read out.

Wolf would rather not have to remember those interrogations in Duisburg that he had been required to attend. Mrs. Bruno had repeatedly asked for the interrogations to be discontinued—surely it was obvious that her husband had had all he could take? In the end Dr. Bruno hadn't even recognized his own handwriting on the slips of paper shown to him. The purpose of the interrogation was to find out from Dr. Bruno whether he had known that the apparatuses and parts he had obtained for Wolf were mere dummies supplied only to hoodwink the Eastern principals. Dr. Bruno had still been able to answer this with an unqualified Yes. Why, then, those delivery problems? Why hadn't he been able, instantly and smoothly, to fulfill the wishes of the Eastern principals as submitted to him by York alias Zieger? Surely this dummy equipment must have been available at any time? So why first only MRS 1 and 4 and only after vehement insistence on the part of the principals Options 2 and 3? Dr. Bruno said that had been his suggestion. As an electronics expert, he had proposed to the work group York—that was what the group allocated to Zieger, who had always used that name on the telephone, was called, a work group consisting of members of various services and bureaus—that deliveries be split up in this way, first for the sake of credibility, since overprompt deliveries might have made the people in East Berlin suspicious, and secondly to test whether the people over there would even notice that the apparatus with Options 1 and 4 wasn't complete.

To what extent, in Dr. Bruno's expert opinion, did the defendant have insight into what he was doing? How did he behave at their meetings in Holland? How did Dr. Bruno become aware that the defendant wished to circumvent Dr. Bruno in order to gain direct access to the Dutch intermediary Kercher and, through him, to the Californian supplier? Again and again the sick man, who was certified as suffering from arteriosclerosis and angina pectoris, had to be confronted with written records of the authorized telephone surveillance, in order to extract a further statement from him.

During those sessions in Duisburg, Wolf had already felt embarrassed at having to listen to the statements of a man who had so outrageously deceived him. Wolf had thought that Dr. Bruno must also feel embarrassed at having to relate, in the presence of the man he had so deceived, how he had gone about it and what he had had in mind. But instead Dr. Bruno seemed actually to cheer up when he described how he had introduced

Kercher from the Netherlands State Security to eager Mr. Zieger as a NATO employee who would provide York with the desired direct contact with California. Weak and stammering as Dr. Bruno was, he did want to savor his triumph over Zieger shortly before he died. Whenever his wife had tried to shield him from further questions, he had said she should allow him this last pleasure. He really had little enough to live for: no alcohol, no cigarettes, no more women, but he should at least be allowed the pleasure of taking a swipe at those fellows in the East before he died.

When he was asked how he, the owner of an electronics trading company, came to be recruited by the West German Federal Criminal Investigation Bureau, he was suddenly too exhausted to give a coherent answer. It was Mr. Bestenhorn who put these questions, his purpose obviously being to undermine the witness's credibility as well as his stature as an expert. Everything in Dr. Bruno's statement might have originated, said Bestenhorn, in anticommunist revenge fantasies. Dr. Bruno had spent years in Soviet prison camps. As a businessman he was practically bankrupt. Even after the first session Mr. Bestenhorn had told Wolf: "You hit on the wrong person there—a bit of luck for you." Nothing useful could have been obtained from him. Who had directed Wolf to him? The people at Information H.Q., said Wolf. Typical, Mr. Bestenhorn had said, in East Berlin they simply believed that anyone who went bankrupt in the West was an ideal collaborator. Those fellows must have a pretty fine index of nincompoops on Normannen-Strasse. The worst part for those people over there was that not only did they believe they would find it easier to do business with bankrupts, which might be correct—no, they're so convinced of the correctness of their own ideology that the moment someone in the West fails in business they regard him as a kind of potential and also potent ally.

The trips that Wolf had made without Dr. Bruno were reconstructed by means of the statements of Dutch secret service men. The superintendent of the Federal Criminal Investigation Bureau, who had been in charge of Wolf's surveillance, presented the court with a picture of splendid cooperation. The German observer had handed the subject under surveillance to his Dutch colleague, who in turn followed him to Venlo and St. Willibrod and back again to the border, where the German colleague had meanwhile filled in the time learning a foreign language. That, too, was revealed by the superintendent. His purpose was probably to point out how ambitious and diligent his men were. The defendant had been a pawn in the hands of the intelligence services. Although himself an eager beaver, making every effort to get closer to the source in order to save his Eastern principals the expense of intermediaries—admirable certainly, his toiling away, even on Saturdays and Sundays, but it was a bit ludicrous too, all this futile expenditure of energy. The defendant's aim: to gain access to a Dutch firm that was close to NATO so that, instead of a special license being required for each import, its general license would enable it to order any high-tech article from the "black list," with no questions asked about the end user.

Of all the choreographers in attendance here, the presiding judge was the gentlest. Although relentless down to the minutest details, as chief choreographer he was more interested in remaining inconspicuous in the proceedings than in being a star above everything and everybody. When he asked the Dutch interpreter whether she had been sworn in by a judge of the County Court, and this self-assertive woman corrected him: "Of the Superior Court!" he merely muttered to himself: "County Court." But she was already brandishing a document taken from her briefcase as evidence that he was wrong and she was right. She slaps the document down in front of him, he reads in a low-keyed, velvety voice: "Sworn in by the President of the County Court, Düsseldorf. Authorized by the President of the Superior Court." And, scarcely raising his voice: "You are welcome to resume your seat, Mrs. Mindermann." The gentle, long-suffering enunciation endowed the name of this ambitious person with an almost devastating quality for its bearer. Wolf experienced a shock.

Nevertheless, his confidence in the presiding judge grew with each passing week. The fact that the judge was willing to devote a separate hearing to Sylvia so that Dorle would never have to confront Sylvia in public and thus possibly have to listen to descriptions or even tape recordings from the Senats-Hotel—surely that was the ultimate in tactfulness! In answering questions from the judge's bench, from the prosecuting attorney, or even from Mr. Bestenhorn, Wolf really spoke only for the benefit of the presiding judge. When, for instance, the prosecuting attorney asked about his childhood in Ottstedt, he took the opportunity of informing the judge that he had spent his childhood with the parents of his prematurely deceased mother, in Leipzig, at Number 7 Rapunzel-Weg. Since his father hadn't moved from East

Prussia until the twenties and his mother came from Leipzig, they had had no relatives in Ottstedt who could have taken care of a child whose father had to go to work. With all this he hadn't told the prosecuting attorney anything, but he hoped to have increased his common ground with the judge.

On being asked by the prosecuting attorney what school he had attended, his answer to her was "ESS" and to the judge, to spare him the anguish of an abbreviation: "Extended Secondary School."

A relationship that almost tempted him to dream: Mr. Bestenhorn, the presiding judge, and himself. True, the prosecuting attorney was a considerable nuisance, but the judge—if Wolf interpreted his reactions correctly—intervened regularly to defuse the attorney's questions and imputations. After one of Wolf's replies she exclaimed in a shrill voice: "That's something entirely new!" whereupon the judge, in a tone that, coming after the piercing female treble, seemed as gentle as swansdown, said: "The defendant has never been asked about this!" Wolf had only to nod. And the way the judge, as long as the public was admitted, avoided any suggestion that Wolf had given himself up! Source protection—Wolf came to appreciate that expression during these weeks.

He was surprised at what he heard about the workings of the intelligence services. The truth is, there are no adults, thought Wolf as he listened to Superintendent Riese speak when the public was excluded. Unwarranted deception, to pretend to children that people thirty years older than they were adults! In order to complete the logic of official intelligence, the superintendent had to add to his public statements that, while it was possible that the people in East Berlin had recognized the material foisted on the accused as being mere toys, they may have allowed the West German intelligence service to believe that they took it for new and instantly serviceable, with the idea of fostering a totally false impression in Western intelligence about the level of East German high-tech electronics. It was true that A-3 Communications for York alias Zieger, which his—the superintendent's—service had been monitoring ever since acquiring the code from Mr. Zieger, at first reported complete satisfaction. Since Zieger's arrest has been publicized there is, of course, no more Brahms to be heard for 17-11-21. But before that Zieger had been highly commended and encouraged to make further trips to Holland. However, that too may be nothing more than red-herring strategy on the part of the Eastern intelligence.

The prosecuting attorney then wanted to know how the defendant felt about this.

"What do you mean?" Wolf asked cautiously in return.

That he had delivered only dummy material, for instance, one item for 750 thousand Swiss francs.

Wolf has no comment.

So the attorney persists: Surely Wolf hadn't doubted even for a second that he was supplying his principals in East Berlin with a useful product of top Western military technology!

Mr. Bestenhorn objected to the insinuations contained in her question. The presiding judge put it to the woman that she was using very colorful language to describe a simple process of ordering and acquiring, whereas in the eyes of a layman there had actually not been much more involved than passing on some abbreviations and numbers and, when necessary, pressing for delivery.

Would Wolf describe himself as a layman in regard to electronics, she now wishes to know?

Yes.

But, as if able to win every competition for precise information, she immediately counters with: Police Interrogation Protocol, Volume III, Sheet 89, the accused: *I did not see myself as a taker of orders. I was motivated by the German situation. The superiority of one side. Particularly in the military/industrial sector, i.e., electronics—that was where the GDR lagged farthest behind. That's why I took it up, familiarized myself with it.* Did he still stand by that?

Yes.

Yet today he calls himself a layman?

Yes.

Didn't he see any contradiction between his present and former self-appraisal?

No.

Well, she says, her tone congealing into sheer scorn, logic is apparently a matter of chance.

"I was afraid you were about to say: 'Logic is apparently not a male attribute,'" said the judge, adding on a note of genuine apology: "I beg your pardon." And, if he might be allowed to comment on the matter, he understood the defendant to mean: he may have known in general what he intended to do, but not in every single case what he was actually doing. Something like that?

Wolf said he hoped this was a description of actions

127

derived not just from his example and hence applying not just to him.

"Does that mean," cried his persecutor, "that you wanted to continue supplying products of top military technology across the border, and that you regret every instance in which you failed to do so?"

Mr. Bestenhorn asked her to withdraw this question since it had already been answered by the fact that Mr. Zieger had given himself up, voluntarily and without pressure.

The persecutor cast doubt on "without pressure." Perhaps the defendant had noticed that he was under surveillance.

Mr. Buhl quickly pushed a sheet of paper over to his young senior partner, who grasped its usefulness at a glance, and said: "I refer you to Interrogation Protocol Volume II, Sheet 144, statement by Zieger, in reply to the question whether he deemed himself to be under surveillance: *'Not at all. I felt absolutely safe. Mainly because my so-called cover was genuine. In other words, whatever could be learned about me in a security check tallied with what I had stated myself when I came to the West and with what I had later confided to suitable persons. Except that fifteen years ago I agreed to work for the State Security Service of the GDR in order to contribute toward diminishing the advantage held by Western military technology. Of course, when someone had just been blown or had switched over, I'd get jittery, too; otherwise never.'* " Was this enough to convince Madam Attorney?

She wanted to know what was really meant by "voluntarily and without pressure."

There had been reasons, said Wolf, but personal ones that were not relevant here.

But Mr. Bestenhorn wanted to hear some of them, merely to refute the prejudice of Madam Attorney that Wolf had given himself up because he suspected he had been found out.

He didn't like revealing personal motives, said Wolf.

"Did you talk to your wife about wanting to give yourself up?"

"No."

"You knew she would agree?"

"Yes."

"Your wife was opposed to what you have called your mediating activities?"

Because Wolf hesitated, Mr. Bestenhorn called out: "Mrs. Zieger?"

Dorle said: "Yes."

Had her husband discontinued these activities on her account?

Dorle said she believed so.

Bestenhorn, emphatically: "Mr. Zieger?"

Wolf said: "Yes."

Apparently that sounded insufficiently unfavorable for the accused, so the persecutor asked whether State Security over there had contacted Wolf after he had slapped his professor.

Yes.

After Wolf had been expelled from the University of Leipzig?

Yes.

And why did the accused slap his professor?

Because he had made fun of the accused's piano playing.

The persecutor: "So you can't take criticism?"

Wolf: "Yes."

The persecutor, surprised: "Thank you."

After such verbal skirmishes, Wolf had the impression that the presiding judge was at the very least more on his side than on the prosecuting attorney's.

The latter devoted herself with particular energy to the obtaining of protocols.

"So there were no other reasons for obtaining the NATO protocols than there were for arranging the electronics deliveries?"

Wolf pretended not to understand the question and looked across to Bestenhorn.

"Well," she went on, "you obtained the electronics, so you said, in the interests of securing peace, didn't you?"

Wolf, hesitantly: "Yes."

"And the lovers' trysts at the Senats-Hotel . . . also exclusively in the interests of securing peace, right?"

Since Wolf didn't answer immediately, she turned to Dorle: "Mrs. Zieger, did you never suspect that your husband might have sought the contact with you simply because you were a secretary at the Ministry of Defense?"

Dorle: "No. I mean, for a while I did, at critical moments, but less and less often, in the end really not at all."

The persecutor: "According to the police protocol, Volume IV, Sheet 98, your husband did not confess his connection with East Berlin to you until after you were married?"

Dorle: "Yes."

The persecutor: "Your reaction?"

130   Dorle: "I'd rather not say."

But the prosecuting attorney persisted, maintaining

that it was important for her to know more precisely how the initiative was distributed between Mr. and Mrs. Zieger. Had Mrs. Zieger known about everything?

"Yes," said Dorle.

She had told her husband through which secretary he could gain access to which protocol?

Yes.

She had known by which means her husband was trying to gain access to the protocols?

Yes.

The persecutor, as if she were tightening a knot: "That shows how concerned you were that the protocols should reach the East! As I see it, you were even more interested than your husband in having the protocols sent across. Your sacrifice was greater than his. Or didn't you care what practical means your husband used to obtain the protocols?"

No.

So it was a sacrifice?

Dorle didn't answer.

For the cause?

No.

But a sacrifice?

"It was very painful," said Dorle.

And why had she brought it upon herself? That pain?

"For my husband," said Dorle.

Surely she could have dissuaded him, given him the choice: herself or the espionage!

Dorle said nothing.

"Did you never consider that?" the persecutor asked.

"No," said Dorle.

131

Bestenhorn intervened: "Your honor, to my mind the

prosecution is playing a game that is no longer in accordance with the concept of marriage in our society and culture. If everything to which one marriage partner consents for the sake of the other partner can be interpreted as collusion, we simply double the number of guilty persons in all criminal proceedings against married couples."

The persecutor said: "It is nevertheless our task to establish whether Mrs. Zieger is to be found guilty as an accessory or merely for condoning a criminal action. Although she did not procure anything herself, she was still active as a contact person. Active, my learned friend! And in the interests of Mrs. Zieger I am concerned with the psychological motivation for that activity. With all due respect to your marriage metaphysics, they are of no help here."

At last the presiding judge spoke up: "Madam Attorney, it can sometimes happen that a woman has greater difficulty in understanding a woman than a man does. When you asked earlier how she had reacted when her husband informed her about his activities, Mrs. Zieger replied that she would rather not say. That answer tells *me* enough. But not you, apparently."

No, said the persecutor: she regarded a wife as something more than a husband's appendage who must say Amen to everything; the sentimental notion of marriage that seemed at the moment to prevail in this room turned the wife into a creature stripped of all responsibility in terms of criminal law.

Neither was she simply detachable, according to the spirit of the law, said the judge.

Fortunately adultery was no longer a punishable offense, said the persecutor; but in this case, where adultery has become a prerequisite for the offense, it was necessary to examine the motivation of both marriage partners thoroughly. "I am not aware that the male capacity for erection can be controlled to such an extent by the political will that sexual desire becomes unnecessary! Or is there in East Berlin some erotic training for agents that renders nature's requirement superfluous? And if not, what motivates a wife to put up with all this?"

"Love," says Dorle.

The persecutor: "That's ... what I was afraid of."

The presiding judge: "That ... was already fairly clear."

The persecutor: "To a man!"

The presiding judge: "So to speak."

After such sessions Wolf was bathed in sweat by the time he entered the green van that transported him to his cell. He would have liked to write the judge a letter of thanks. He must rescue the judge from the clutches of the prosecuting attorney. Was he succeeding? Was the relationship still as it had been the first day?

The judge was always agreeable, always helpful, always precise, never sarcastic, never overbearing, never mean, but, as agreeable as he was, always concentrated on the issue. He was genuinely concerned with the issue. With nothing but the issue. But that was what Wolf wanted, wasn't it? That was why he felt that Mr. Bestenhorn's somewhat sentimental role-invention had to be supplemented by objectivity and veracity. In the West, Wolf had discovered how much of the East had been lost here. He had experienced the growing coldness toward everything the two parts had in common, as well as the crass want of understanding, the overweening insensitivity and arrogance toward what was happening in the GDR. The two parts reverberated with mutual want of understanding. Each wanted to outdo the other in rejection. Each wished to lay claim to more historical justification, thereby relegating the other to proportionately less. Each vied with the other as an ardent shield-bearer for the camp to which it had been allocated. Each wanted to be a model student in its own school. In this way each had developed hostility toward the other as the most vital ingredient of its self-awareness.

And this was what Wolf wanted to remedy, in a precarious field—that of armaments. And he is glad to reveal every detail. All things considered, they cannot refute his account of himself and his actions here. And he is not interested in any further scheming and plotting. He is prepared, if that is criminal, to be punished. But if his aims and his actions are criminal, then the true crime is what made him a criminal: the partition of Germany and its continuation and accentuation by all possible means. That was it. And that was what he was trying to convey in all his replies, directed as they were at the presiding judge, a man of his own age whose intonation sounded East Prussian to him. In other words, although of his own age, the judge reminded him quite simply of his father.

Never mind what kind of antenna system, this or another; never mind whether the black hollow coils supplied twelve or forty gigaherz, or whether Superintendent Riese of the Federal Criminal Investigation Bureau made himself out to be the savior of the Republic;

never mind how comical the accused appeared as he dangled from the threads of the security services: his failure was the very thing he did not want turned into his chief merit; he wanted to stand by his cause. The presiding judge would know how to appreciate that, even if he did perhaps regard the cause as a lost one. As indeed it was. His own and the larger one. But Wolf didn't consider himself lost in a lost cause. He was not attracted by the obtuseness of those who are quick to declare everything lost and thus make of themselves winners.

All negative attitudes seemed to him weak. Everything that failed to link up with history as a whole seemed to him lifeless. Even the most brilliant arguments, the purest theses, the most sensitive points of view—everything that did not invoke history as a whole, everything that strove to dissociate itself from that history, everything that sought only its own advantage, a source of rejoicing to the rest of the world, an ingenious subject for abstract experimentation: all this might be admired, by each side in its own way, as a model of German ingenuity, but Wolf wanted the whole, even if it were a lost whole. That was it.

His only hope was the presiding judge. Actually he should have withdrawn his brief from Mr. Bestenhorn; after the very first consultation he should have parted company with him. Mr. Bestenhorn had said that of course he was in favor of Wolf's appearing before the court as a victim of the German partition; Wolf's history was enough to suggest that. But to speak of a political motivation would be downright damaging. Pointless, too. No one here still believed in the reunification of these

German states. Of course, there was still this or that official lip service, constitutional cant, but there was no way of envisioning a German reunion and, more important still, not the slightest demand for it. "We don't feel deprived," he said. He didn't feel deprived. This doesn't mean that for a time there won't still be victims of this partition. Take Wolf Zieger. That should be put to use. Even exploited. Even Wolf's pathetic notion of achieving a balance between the unequal parts can be turned to account. But with caution, please. As the fantasy of an emigrant damaged by his past experiences, yes! But not, please, as a politically reasonable plan of action. Not, please, as something genuinely desired. . . .

In Mr. Bestenhorn's opinion it wasn't necessary for Wolf to try to fool him, his helper. But, if one wishes to retain one's credibility, one cannot expect a court to believe that Wolf supplied the East with knowledge and equipment for the sole purpose of bringing the two parts of Germany closer together. It must not, it simply cannot, be claimed that Wolf personally wished to bring about the reunification of the two German states. "No one is going to accept that from you!" Bestenhorn had protested.

Wolf told Mr. Bestenhorn to formulate everything as he saw fit. Mr. Bestenhorn had allowed himself to be reconciled. Obviously Mr. Bestenhorn had taken everything Wolf had said about this German malaise for a concoction. Bypass Mr. Bestenhorn, head straight for the presiding judge! That was Wolf's plan. The judge must find out for himself that Wolf was more than what Bestenhorn was making of him. On the other hand, in Bestenhorn he sensed utter hopelessness. His cause was lost.

Bestenhorn was right. No one makes a completely lost cause his own: Wolf wasn't enough of a clown for that. He would mention it once more in court. Very cautiously. Then never again. Dorle, you can be sure of that. Never, never again. He saw his father nodding. His father had also spoken less and less whenever he came to visit them. Once he had said: "Unbelievable, what they're doing to the people. That they have the nerve! That they have the nerve to do that!"

So, this uncontrollably widening gap—what was there left for him to do, and how? Dorle was pregnant. Surely that's enough. No. But. . . . He felt as if he were on a merry-go-round. Faster and faster.

18

Whenever Dorle was allowed to visit Wolf, they sat silently facing each other, separated by thick panes of glass, connected by intercoms, yet slightly less able to feel alone than the other couples who, Wolf thought, simply seemed livelier. "Dorle," he said, "say something—we can't let the time go by without saying something—how are you feeling, is everything all right?" "The doctor says Yes," said Dorle. "It's fantastic, isn't it, Dorle," said Wolf. "How about a laugh? I love the way you laugh. It'd be good for the baby. Your diaphragm will collapse on his head if you never laugh. D'you hear? Laugh, can't you? For the baby's sake. I want to have a healthy child when I get out, let me tell you. Laugh, *please*! It's all just a circus here anyway. Life will begin in Strümpfelbach. Is that clear? Tell your brother: I'm still studying management models. Productivity control. I'll ruin his outfit within a few months. With my own model. And you'll send me all my music. And one of those Yamaha keyboards for practicing. Costs less than two hundred marks. In three years at most I'll come and give you a concert that'll be right out of this world."

Dorle said nothing.

"Are you listening, Dorle?"

Dorle said: "Yes, Wolf."

Wolf said: "And if they try to contact you, from over there, about exchange and all that . . . you know what to do."

He made a gesture of complete dismissal.

As soon as he was back in his cell he felt annoyed; he sat down and wrote ten pages. To Dorle. Obviously the two of them could not adapt to the prison administration's method of allowing them to speak to each other.

Toward Dorle, Wolf adopted an attitude that he would like to have had, that he wanted to practice. He played the part of someone who simply puts behind him whatever can happen to him now. One can keep that up for two, maybe three years. Really. Inner fortitude, a calm that cannot be reached by nerves. It does exist, this fortitude, this calm. If you have no other choice. Prove it. Subside. To a degree that you yourself wouldn't have thought possible. Practice inaccessibility. Rehearse inaccessibility until you have achieved a mood that cannot be torn to shreds by every footstep that approaches your door. Above all, Dorle must take the impression with her: you have resources of strength that until now you have been unaware of.

Especially on Saturdays and Sundays he felt how weak he was, how much he still had to learn. What he missed was the people, the court. He missed the presiding judge: why didn't he come to see him during the weekend? Mr.

Bestenhorn had said the judge wanted the case finished by Christmas. The verdict, then the celebration! If you please. Whenever Wolf found himself getting tense in a way he didn't like, he would ask himself sharply, almost audibly: Is anything hurting you at the moment? No. So get off my back, will you? That meant: leave me alone. You are very, very well off.

When totally unable to cope with his inner tension, he would abandon himself to looking out the little window placed high up in the wall. A treetop reached up to his square of window. Over the weeks, this treetop has lost almost all its leaves. Some of the branches sway, others remain still. Nothing is clearer than the fact that it is afternoon. This is conveyed by the treetop with the swaying and the motionless branches: afternoon in the fall. The wind seems to be roaming about, is in no hurry. You have surrendered to it. You sway, remain still. Neither waiting nor not-waiting. History is over for you. It wasn't much. Very little.

19

When the time came for the concluding arguments, there were more spectators again. As Wolf was escorted to his place, he tried not to take notice of the public area and the spectators, but as soon as he was seated it did go through his mind that, in spite of not looking, he had seen Mr. Ujfalussy and Dr. Meissner.

As long as the prosecuting attorney was speaking, Wolf did not move. He stared in front of him. He concentrated on what he was hearing. The reddish brown, unpatterned varnish of his table helped. Although during the days and weeks of the presentation of evidence he had become accustomed to the unpleasant thought process and delivery of this lady—for that's what she was, a lady and nothing more—in her summation and request for sentencing she outdid herself. He realized that he was totally unprepared. The sweat ran down from his armpits and grew cold on his hips. To think that anyone could be allowed to speak like that about another person! There is probably nothing less thoughtful in the whole world than a prosecuting attorney. To think that anyone would so grossly exaggerate this role assigned to her by law! To think that a person wouldn't be embarrassed to elevate herself so greatly over another person! How come she knew everything better? Why doesn't a prosecutor's office ask itself whether it isn't at least slightly in tune to the reality and nature of the defendant? He wished he could meet this woman someday, outside. While she was holding forth in the courtroom, he saw her outside, saw himself walking toward her and saw her fear of him, and then he walked past her. But not without spitting at her feet. No, he hadn't done that. Inaccessibility, come to his aid! A person like that must simply not exist for him. A person who plays a power role, one that is allotted to her by society, with such blatant self-involvement needs to be forgotten. If only he had some earplugs. . . .

And then, when she applied for the sentence—seven and a half years—he couldn't keep his eyes on the table in front of him. His head jerked up. He seemed to have heard Dorle. A scream. He looked across to the persecutor. She looked at him. She savored this exchange. He had to endure her gaze. She held the power. He acknowledged that in his gaze. She had destroyed him. She had surpassed everything he had been thinking about her and fearing from her. Two years for Dorle. Mr. Bestenhorn and Buhl escorted him out, whispering and talking simultaneously. Nothing but a theatrical bluff, that's all that woman was capable of. Wolf had managed to meet Dorle's eyes before leaving the courtroom. The attorneys pumped him up. With hope. Don't worry, Mr. Zieger. On Monday it's Mr. Bestenhorn's turn. And then Wolf himself. If he feels like it. He can think about it over the weekend.

Wolf sat in the cell that had already come to feel like his room, and he was glad to be alone. Seven and a half years . . . he wanted to be left alone with that. He didn't want to speak to anybody about that. He was quite sure that the prosecuting attorney didn't have a relative who had been sentenced to seven and a half years. Probably all prosecuting attorneys come from the same families. As do the condemned. The former always punish and the latter are always punished. Anything else would be unthinkable. How could anyone who has any idea of the effect: seven and a half years! How could such a person even demand such a sentence? Division of labor, that's the prerequisite for such a demand. How about a student of statistics taking a ten-year period and calculating whether that is *not* the case! How many of the condemned come from families that produce those who condemn? And vice versa: how many of those who condemn come from families that produce the condemned? A cleaner separation than this is to be found nowhere else. And there is nothing that this has less to do with than heredity. The families whose background always supplies them with more justification than they need for themselves produce those who condemn. If from childhood on one has more right than is needed for one's own justification, one uses the surplus to condemn others. . . .

Wolf sensed that he had to let go. Not look for any resistance to what now had to come out. Now he will speak. He will instruct Mr. Bestenhorn to emphasize clearly in his summation that the accused did not wish to be exchanged, the accused wished to remain in the West, have a family, a private life—he couldn't care less about Germany and all that. Everything he had ever wanted, planned, done that did not arise from his personal, private needs was error, garbage, pure nonsense. Apart from eating, drinking, sleeping, and what he did with Dorle—thus, the defendant—there was really nothing. Let everything desirous of rising above that go to hell. He had a definite sensation that something was leaving him. That's how it must be when the blood was being sucked out of one's veins. For the first time a private person. A shell resounding with emptiness. He was scared. Was he now also halved? At last. Be glad. Able to compete at last. Take a deep breath. . . .

Wolf had the feeling he was slipping. He could no longer hold on to anything. That woman had finished him. That's how weak he was. He wouldn't have imagined that. Luckily he was alone. He could feel his eyes brimming over, which helped. But it seemed a bit exaggerated. He could do something about that. It's only water, he told himself. Those aren't tears. He said it to that woman, who had always walked toward her seat with her overlong strides and her overwide skirts. Not tears, madam. Just water. . . .

Being helpless is pretty exhausting. Having always to think of the person who has reduced one to this condition is the worst part. That is the spice of exerting power. That's what she lives on. The person kicked concentrates on nothing but the kick. And thus on the kicker. Just as well that woman couldn't see how she dominated him now. Don't wonder what she's doing at this moment. One thing is sure, she's not thinking of you. Perhaps right now she is accepting compliments for her summation. Even then she's thinking not about Wolf Zieger but only about herself. After all, everyone does everything for himself. That's almost a consolation. Wolf

Zieger is of little concern to her. She has to give a fantastic prosecuting address, and for that of course she
needs an accused. So he really has no reason to feel personally singled out let alone persecuted by her. It wasn't
even certain whether she had carried on the legal business of prosecution with such vehemence for the sake
of the law, of society; the only certainty was that she
had enjoyed holding forth like that. She had seemed fantastic to herself. One could sense that. Even when her
words were solemn and restrained. Even when she felt
nothing but concern for the greater good, she was still
the fantastic person who felt that concern. Where, then,
was the difference between her and the public behavior
of East German Minister of Justice Hilde Benjamin,
known there as the Red Guillotine!

Wouldn't it be better to develop computers that can
be fed with the entire evidence, after which a demand
for a sentence comes out? Out of the prosecuting attorney's computer! Then the defense computer replies. The
judge's computer renders judgment. No, at that point
Wolf put the brakes on his imagination. He did not want
to have to do without the presiding judge. In that quar-
ter there was an indication of emotional capacity, hence
understanding, hence hope. Once again Wolf's thoughts
were devoted extensively, even immoderately, to the
presiding judge.

When on Monday Wolf rose from his seat in honor of
the panel's entry and observed the expected little pla-
catory gestures on the part of the presiding judge, he
felt almost happy. Not a glance toward the red-haired
lady. When a presiding judge of such stature entered,   145
she was, after all, practically demolished. A painted pup-

pet of justice, that's all she was. Of no consequence. So much for her.

But now Mr. Bestenhorn had started to speak. Shortly before the session Wolf had handed him his capitulation: Mr. Bestenhorn may announce, in language as loud and flowery as he likes and as his standing will permit, that the accused does not wish to be exchanged because he wishes to remain in the West, in the West, in the West. . . . Here the needle got stuck in the record.

Mr. Bestenhorn spoke as well as one had a right to expect of him: ". . . But, your honors, the determination of guilt in a case of treason . . . the very word treason, your honors, what images does that evoke! Must not each one of us, no matter how convinced he is of knowing the flow of his emotion, must not each one of us admit to prejudice toward that loaded word? Who can claim to be unprejudiced toward that word? Who can hope to ascribe only a factual connotation to that word? A person may be as advanced as he likes: each one of us is still in the shadow of a tradition in which a military ruling clique stylized its murderous trade as sacred to the nation and punished with death and loathing any who violated that chauvinistic taboo. The tone of indignation with which the prosecution has demanded sentences approaching the maximum in our case, also for the sake of deterrence—that tone, your honors, is totally inappropriate in our day, particularly in a divided Germany and in view of the history and personality of the defendant. We have to consider the case of Wolfgang Zieger as if there had never been and could never be a similar one. Deterrence at his expense . . . fortunately a citizen of our society does not have to tolerate that. As a nom de guerre the defendant chose a name from the most honorable Prussian tradition: York von Wartenburg. At a critical moment that venerated Prussian general concluded the Treaty of Tauroggen with the Russians in order to demonstrate to his king that Prussia must not remain Napoleon's vassal throughout eternity. Opinions may differ about personalities who obey their own conscience more than they do the law of the land; but there is one thing that should be avoided: denigrating their motives on principle, as it were. Our political leaders can bring only lip service to bear on the tragedy of divided Germany.

"Wolfgang Zieger could not endure this state of affairs," Bestenhorn went on. "The law meant less to him than the Fatherland. All those who have comfortably settled down in the two German fragments may smile or laugh at that. I lost my trendy West German complacency when I came to know the seriousness and dedication that motivated the defendant in what our laws call treason. He simply refused to acknowledge the German partition. That is his crime. My views on the German partition certainly differ from those of the defendant; I also know—we all know—that, with what he romantically calls scouting activities, he can have had no thought of politics much less of *Realpolitik,* but it was inevitable that his life history should bring him to where he is now: in the dock. How did Talleyrand put it? *La trahison—c'est une question du temps. . . .*"

Bestenhorn went to great lengths in describing the minimal damage that had been inflicted by the defendant as certified by the experts. For this, the appropriate judgment would not be a sentence approaching the maximum but rather acquittal. If indeed damage had not also been caused in the political sphere. That damage, if we sincerely attempt to understand the defendant in his life story and personality, would most certainly be expiated by two years' imprisonment.

The co-defendant Mrs. Doris Zieger must be acquitted. Her participation cannot be assessed as complicity. In the eyes of the law, a deed is deemed to have been perpetrated jointly only when each of the participants has willed the deed as his own. Only in such cases can the action of the one be ascribed also to the other. It is beyond doubt that such is not the case here. . . .

Wolf no longer objected to the simplifications that Mr. Bestenhorn had allowed to congeal into ponderous images.

When the presiding judge asked whether Wolf wished to exercise his right to be the last to speak before the court withdrew to render judgment, Wolf rose and looked the judge in the eye. They were about ten feet apart. This time the judge could not avoid Wolf's eyes. Wolf managed to maintain his gaze for quite a while. There flashed through his mind what he now had to say. Heidelberg, the Old Town, four or five years ago: he had been showing the city to a group of Japanese engineers. Suddenly one of the group hurries over to a young woman pushing a bicycle; he calls to the others to join him, they want to take a picture of this young woman with her ancient bicycle, an NSU bicycle, to judge by its appearance a product more of nature than of industry. The young woman had come with this bicycle years ago from the GDR; the Japanese invite the young woman, who looks spunky and wistful and attractive, to join them in a wine tavern. There she tells them about Klein-Glienicke, where she grew up. At that time the Wall was still only a wooden fence, garnished with barbed wire. The East German kids used to climb up the fence and, when they got to the top, make Eastern faces for Western tourists; yes, that's what they had called it: making Eastern faces, which meant pulling down the corners of their mouths and making their eyes bulge as hideously as possible. As a result, oranges, bananas, and packages of chewing gum would be thrown across, until the People's Police arrived and put an end to the performance. That, your honor, is how the roles are distributed in the tragicomedy that is Germany. Should you doubt the truth of this theatrical version of the German partition, you can check it out. The source is not protected and is no doubt still available: Elke Wehr, Heidelberg. The Japanese were thrilled with her. Wolf had arranged with Elke Wehr to let her know whenever he was showing Japanese around Heidelberg. He wanted to integrate her into his program for Japanese. . . . The presiding judge repeated his question as to whether Wolf wished to exercise his right to have the last word. If you say nothing, you can't say anything wrong, thought Wolf, and replied: No.

Dorle didn't wish to say anything either, so the session came to a close. Wolf felt that the exchange of looks between him and the judge had been important. Far more important than having the last word. Wolf had poured his entire confidence in the judge into that one look. In fact, much more. Himself. Stripped of protection, Wolf had looked at the judge. Put himself at his mercy. But he felt that the judge had understood him.

20

WOLF HAD TOLD himself all he could to remain calm. It hadn't helped. Apparently he was a kind of tightly wound spring. The days and weeks of the preliminary hearings and the days and weeks of the trial itself seemed to have had only the one inexorable effect: to wind him up like a spring. He felt so tense that he was afraid he would suddenly yell something or do something. Something to release that tension. But he also knew that he wouldn't yell anything or do anything as long as the presiding judge had not spoken. Hadn't he been living throughout these weeks and months in anticipation of this moment? Living only for this moment? It was high time to tell himself that, no matter what this presiding judge would have to say, he would go on living. And whatever this judge would decree, he, Wolf Zieger, would survive. Listen to him, man. He's already speaking. And he's speaking for you. And just the way you expected. Expected of him. At last the tension is released.

The way the judge was speaking tempted Wolf to look

across to the prosecuting attorney. Either gloatingly or contemptuously. But he controlled himself. He didn't look at the judge either. Certainly not now. It would have been embarrassing to meet the judge's eye just when the latter was speaking of him with so much understanding, while he was at last putting back into place the circumstances that the prosecuting attorney had so maliciously displaced. And how! In no series of paragraphs was the sentencing more closely bound to the actual damage caused than in Paragraphs 94 to 99. If there was any place where motives were secondary to the actual deed, then it was here. Nowhere was there less excuse for giving the intention priority over the deed. Not that he, the judge, subscribed to the attempt at justification put forward by the defendant and so passionately depicted by the defense: that everything had been done solely to secure peace in this unhappily divided country. Scout for peace, intermediary between German extremes ... those were politically romantic turns of speech that the court could not accept for purposes of limiting criminal liability. But then what the defendant, as the agent he was, had accomplished, was negligible, regardless of his motives. Perhaps espionage was the only field in which lack of success could redound to a person's advantage. And when it came to lack of success this agent was scarcely to be surpassed.

Although Wolf was none too pleased to hear this, he told himself that the judge must have chosen this route as the most favorable for Wolf. Wolf was conscious of being made to look ridiculous, but rather two hours of looking ridiculous than seven and a half years in prison. This was not the time to be oversensitive. And the judge was already qualifying Wolf's lack of success. The defendant had not done nothing. In obtaining political and strategic knowledge, he had unquestionably been in a position to damage the security of the Federal Republic.

At this point the judge's tone grew somewhat firmer. Wolf listened, was a little shocked, was a little more shocked and a little more, until he felt stunned. He felt nothing anymore. Without any show of emotion but quite relentlessly, the judge described how much more successful Wolf Zieger had been in obtaining NATO protocols and how much damage he had caused thereby. Wolf listened desperately for East Prussian sounds and coloration in the judge's pronunciation. Had it all been only his imagination? The judge would acknowledge absolutely nothing but the written law of this Republic, which had to be protected by the application of this law to the facts of the case. Protected from an East that had nothing but evil intentions vis-à-vis this Republic. The judge did not need the melodrama resorted to by the prosecuting attorney. He spoke from deep conviction, with the utmost discernment. There was no possibility of doubt. This state is everything it can and should be. Sovereign and definitive. It is a crime to pass on the knowledge that this state has accumulated, in alliance with others, to countries whose declared aim it is to harm our state. He spoke of the level of history that one must occupy. Of the irreversibility of history. Of the crime of personal presumption. Whether adventurism, resentment, vicissitudes of life, or self-assertiveness was the deciding factor is not for him to decide. What counts is the effect. And what counts is the manner in which the secret material was procured. That had been heinous and reprehensible. The method by which the defendant—who is trying to exonerate himself with illusions of idealism—recruited his wife and the co-defendant Sylvia Wellershoff for his criminal purposes by exploiting their emotions, was unscrupulous to the highest degree. . . .

Wolf had the feeling he was hearing the voice from another room. Had his earlids fallen shut? Some kind of protective mechanism had come into play. He was no longer there. He looked straight ahead, but he saw nothing. He was blind and deaf. The world had shrunk to a single voice. That of the presiding judge. Dorle and Sylvia, nine months' probation. Wolf, five years.

As in a sudden cacophonous, tumultuous accident, he could no longer take anything in. Only when he was back in his cell did he gradually come to. Only after he had wept. For hours. For a whole night. Only when he was so exhausted that he could remain lying on his bed. Had to. Only when he could no longer move at all, much less defend himself, did he begin to visualize the conclusion of the court performance. But, as after an accident, whole phases were blank. He made no effort to recall what was lost.

Mr. Buhl and Mr. Bestenhorn tried to raise his spirits. In the room he had always waited in before and after the sessions. First Mr. Buhl. "A star jurist," said Mr. Buhl, almost panting with envy and hatred and admiration and contempt, "there you have the star jurist. There's no way you can get close to him. A man like that wipes the floor with you, however and whenever it suits him. There's a saying, Mr. Zieger, a Danish saying: with judges and drunks you never know which way they'll lurch. . . ." At that point Bestenhorn came charging in: "No, no, no! Never fear, Zieger, we'll throw it right back at him! Buhl, you've made a note of the grounds for an appeal?" Buhl crisply confirmed that he had. Buhl is a specialist in preparing appeals. "Never fear, Zieger, he won't get away with that. Five years— he must be off his rocker! Just what one would expect of an opportunist! He's aiming to become chief justice before he's forty. Clear as day. Ingratiate himself. With a few Party friends. Justice that courts admiration, that's what it is. Look at me, you can rely on me. Never fear, Zieger, he won't get away with it. You can bet on that, Zieger. And as long as the appeal is under way, you can have a good life in remand custody. All I'm saying is: Chin up, Zieger, I'll take care of that presiding judge. Just you wait and see!"

Then Wolf is sitting in the green van. He is not told what they are waiting for. But he can look out. Although through little barred windows. Now he sees Dorle coming out of the rear entrance of the superior court. And two men had been standing there all the time. Not speaking to each other, although, as it turns out, they have both been waiting for Dorle. Dr. Meissner and Dorle's brother. They both rush toward Dorle; Dr. Meissner is the first to reach her. A confab. Then Dr. Meissner walks to his car, walking as if he had just received a beating. But then he always did walk like that. Dr. Meissner has been disciplined by being transferred to the Ministry of Finance. His wife is pregnant again. All this is quite apparent, even if one hadn't been told, just from watching Dr. Meissner cross the parking lot. He walks as if at each step he had to drag his feet out of a leaden mire. Dorle is following Dr. Meissner with her eyes. She can't help him. Dieter's eyes are also following Dr. Meissner, but differently. He's probably saying, as he watches Dr. Meissner: "Slimy bastard."

Dieter and Dorle are talking to each other. Dieter points to the van. They come closer. But before they reach it, two more figures emerge from the rear entrance. Sylvia and blond-bearded Dominick. Sylvia walks quickly toward her car. Dominick runs after her. She sits down at the wheel. He obviously wants to be taken along. Sylvia slams the door in his face and drives off. Dominick leaves the parking lot very slowly. Dorle and Dieter stop a few yards away from the van. They look up at Wolf. Wolf could ask his guard to open the door, but the man is probably not allowed to do that.

Now three figures emerge from the rear entrance. Laughing and chatting they walk toward their cars, which are parked close together: the prosecuting attorney, Mr. Bestenhorn, and the presiding judge. The prosecuting attorney is walking between the two men. The judge is the shortest, the slightest. His head looks too big for his body, too heavy. He holds it tilted either forward or to one side. Apparently he is quite unable to hold his head straight. They are walking toward their cars. Pause for cordial handshakes. The two men go to their BMWs. Between the BMWs, the prosecuting attorney's Porsche. When she is already seated in her car, the judge goes over to her for a last word. Now Mr. Bestenhorn must also join them once again. But then they are in agreement and can drive out, one behind the other, onto the street. They all turn in the same direction.

Now Mr. Buhl comes out too. He waves to Wolf before squeezing into his VW. Suddenly it dawns on Wolf: the judge and Mr. Bestenhorn must also have seen or at least noticed the green van with the barred windows. But it is unthinkable for them to have waved to Wolf the way Buhl the chainsmoker had. Dieter and Dorle are still standing there, hesitating to come any closer. When two police officers get into the front seat of the prison van, Dorle takes another two steps, but the van is already moving off. Dorle and Dieter wave until Wolf can no longer see them. Dorle has called out something that, to judge by her lip movements, might have been: "See you soon!"

Wolf saw the stack of paper on his table, the writing materials. He sat down at the table. He would write to Dorle. He would write every day to Dorle. Until he was exhausted. He would tell her his life story. For the first time.

He must start with the afternoon in Giessen when he had left the refugee reception center for the first time and gone into town, to a café. Hardly had he sat down when a young woman seated herself at the same little table, straight across from him. She took care not to meet his eyes: if she *had* looked at him he might have believed that she hadn't chosen his table by chance. But more than likely she hadn't even been trying not to meet his eyes. Probably she hadn't even noticed that someone else was sitting there. Well, noticed perhaps, the way one notices a wastebasket when one doesn't happen to need one. He felt compelled to get up, quickly pay his bill, and hurry back to the center.

He could still hear her voice as she ordered a cup of coffee. It had Swabian overtones. The first time he heard

Dorle speak he had been reminded of that girl in Giessen. This is what he wanted to tell Dorle about now.

There was also a letter from Sylvia on the table: more of a note than a letter. Buhl had appointed himself messenger between Sylvia and Wolf. Wolf had written to her that there must be no further communication between them. But he had written in such a way that she could still reply, whereupon he had written her a still more discouraging letter, although again not discouraging enough. Now he realized: he would never be able to write to Sylvia in such a way that she wouldn't write back. Don't write at all. Silence. Finish. But he couldn't resist drawing her last note out of the envelope again and reading the single sentence: *I touch myself in the bathtub, every day at seven, promise me you'll concentrate on that because I need you, at seven and always, Your Sylvia.* He tore the note up into tiny shreds. That had now become possible. The unrelenting judge had separated him from all human beings. Not from Dorle. Everything except Dorle was unimportant. He must establish a connection to Dorle. How much strength had flowed from those last seconds when he had seen Dorle, on the parking lot behind the courthouse! With what strength she had stood there, beside Dieter! He felt one with her. Between him and Dorle there could be no tragedy. Because she had that strength. She had survived those terrible years. She had put her trust in something that hadn't even existed yet. It was only through her trust that she had created in him what she could trust in. She was a creator. That's right. His creator. He would now write to her for years. What he had never been able to say to her he might now be able to write to her.

He sensed a new ambition. This did seem somewhat

comical to him at the moment, but also familiar. He knew himself. When something surfaced in him, he could not remain calm. Discretion has never been his forte. He always needs something for which he can do more than can conceivably be expected. And in the coming years—two or three, say—he needs something that he can exaggerate more than he has ever exaggerated anything. A project to end all projects is what he needs. He mustn't drop out of the world in this cell. At some point his eyes will no longer smart from constant wiping and drying. At some point he will put even the presiding judge behind him. When in his mind's eye he has looked at the judge's words and gestures for the thousandth time as if at some vicious educational film, that film will simply stop reeling off inside his head. Probably it will be months before he can hope to understand the judge even slightly. First he must take back, pulverize, destroy, forget everything he had imputed to him in order to expect it from him later. A task that is vital to him. Only when he can think of the judge as he thinks of Mr. Bestenhorn or the prosecuting attorney—only then can he begin to write calmly to Dorle. Until then only hurried letters, loving notes, *cris de cœur*, words of encouragement. For the time being it is unimaginable that he should ever be able to think of the presiding judge calmly. He probably loved the judge. Had placed himself entirely in his hands and so on. And the judge noticed nothing of all this. He simply did his job like a surgeon who doesn't need to be interested in the person under his knife. Buhl blamed everything on the star jurist. Bestenhorn offered career speculation as an explanation. To Wolf such explanations mean nothing. The judge has blue eyes, a steep, domed forehead. A large mouth. A noticeable dimple in his left cheek. Hands that seem reluctant to obey him. An intonation reminiscent—Wolf is sure—of East Prussia. . . .

At first, Wolf could only reconstruct events letter by letter; comprehension was beyond him. That calm identifying with the West German state! A German judge. Wolf would immediately understand that in the case of a French, a Swedish, an Italian judge. But in Germany . . . This judge had shown him how one can live in a part as if it were the whole. A German judge. . . . Wolf longed to be able to forget the presiding judge.

The worst part now will always be waking up. You wake up, and the first thing that intrudes upon your mind is the worst: the presiding judge. Once he has put the judge behind him he can start writing to Dorle. Then nothing more will inhibit him. Then he will let himself be driven by his new ambition: Dorle and Wolf, that must become a relationship such as has never before existed between human beings. That's how high he must aim. He must be obsessed with ambition, otherwise he'll never get through these two or three years. And nowhere but in Dorle can he find the strength. A presiding judge relegated to his natural or social or historical context—then off to Dorle! An infinite drawing close to another person. That's what he wants; that's what he'll accomplish. By the time he leaves the cell Dorle will know him, from all he will have written her, better than anyone has ever known another person. That will, he believes, when they are together again, be something on which they can both live. To put it mildly. In reality it will, of course, be much more and much much more beautiful than he can now imagine. And that's a good thing. Otherwise he wouldn't be able to bear this separation. He has always been living in separations, until now. All his energy and labors had been devoted to overcoming a separation. For the first time he was so ... harshly separated. So vulnerable through separation. He mustn't postpone anything. He had to write to Dorle immediately. Now. Dearest Dorle, he wrote, and with this simple salutation he already had the feeling that he was starting, that he was taking off, and wouldn't land again for a long time.